I0587919

PRAISE FOR
The Exit Plan & Other Stories

"I was captivated by not only the imagination but also the spiritual depth that Pia Orleane has woven throughout all of her short stories. The elements of self-awareness and personal growth are seen in many ways in the themes she has created. Her understanding of freedom and the stepping away from limitations is the magic ingredient that permeates all of her tales."

—Cullen Baird Smith,
Internationally Recognized Author and Lecturer

"If you feel sad, powerless, or in any way restricted in your life here on Earth, this book is your key to freedom. In a gentle and loving way, Pia Orleane shares the magic of transformation with the reader. Here we have the author's shining heart empowering us to return to our true nature. In short, *Exit Plan* is educational, transformational, and simply magical!"

—Vineta Svelch,
Linguist, Translator, and Editor

Exit Plan

and other Short Stories

*Stories from Love & Light
based on Laarkmaa's Wisdom
from the Stars™,*

*Mother Mary, Mary Magdalene,
Angels, Fairies, & Other Voices
from Light*

Pia Orleane, Ph.D.

Onewater Press
Santa Fe, NM

Exit Plan and Other Short Stories
Pia Orleane, Ph.D.

Copyright © 2021 Pia Orleane, Ph.D.
Published by: Onewater Press
369 Montezuma Avenue, Suite 525
Santa Fe, NM 87501

Order Books through booksellers,
or through Onewater Press at www.piaorleane.com

The information contained in this book is intended to educate, delight,
and expand your awareness. These stories are entirely a work of fiction.
The names, characters, incidents portrayed in these stories are the work
of the author's originality. They were written to inspire your imagination
and broaden your perspective in your quest for spiritual, emotional,
and physical well-being.

Original Cover Artwork by Anna Karmaz
Cover and Interior design by Rebecca Finkle, FPGD.com
Author Photo by Judith Pavlik

Printed in the United States of America
Softcover ISBN 978-1-7367035-8-8
eBook ISBN 978-1-7367035-7-1
audiobook ISBN 978-1-7367035-0-2

Library of Congress Control Number: data on file

To Cullen, who has enriched my life in all dimensions beyond measure. Without your love, there would be no stories.

To the Pleiadian group, Laarkmaa, who shares their cosmic perspective with love. To Mother Mary, Mary Magdalene, and The Voice, who bring us grace, strength, and wisdom. To the Yellow People, the Elders in the Water, the Angelic and Fairy beings who have taught me about magic all of my life. To Antonis and Moira, and to countless others who have brought me healing, remembrance, and trust. Thank you for being on this journey with me.

And to my readers, many of whom have been following Laarkmaa's Pleiadian wisdom for years! Thank you for having the courage to reach beyond what you believed was possible.

This book is intended to inspire, uplift, and shed light on the human journey. Each of these stories is based upon my resonance with the perspectives that Laarkmaa and other Voices From Light have shared with Cullen and me through the years as they encourage all of us to change our beliefs, raise our vibrations, and step into becoming Cosmic Citizens. Some of these stories come from experiences others have shared with us. Some come from our own experiences and knowing. And some, based upon concepts Laarkmaa or others have been instilling into the hearts and minds of evolving human consciousness, are simply fiction at this time.

Or are they?

Contents

Foreword

If you feel sad, powerless, or in any way restricted in your life here on Earth, this book is your key to freedom. If you focus on love and light and see everything that happens around you simply as experiences, this book will assure you that you have your ticket to freedom in your hand. We always have a choice as long as we live in Duality here on Earth. When we are consciously weaving love and light into our reality, magic happens.

Each story helps us to re-remember who we are by encouraging us to choose love instead of fear. In a gentle and loving way, Pia Orleane shares the magic of transformation with the reader. The eloquent language of the author conjures up an image of a fairy stepping out of every story touching the reader with her magic wand and saying, "Do You remember Who You Are now?"

As a true eye-opener, the book shows us reality as it is and how to obtain our own freedom. If your heart is full of love and light, you will recognize the truth and resonate with the idea of an exit plan to escape the artificial way of living that exists in today's techno-world. One heart is enough to show the way for others to follow, and here we have the author's shining heart empowering us to return to our true nature. In short, *Exit Plan* is educational, transformational and simply magical!

—Vineta Svelch
Linguist, Translator, and Editor

Exit
Plan

and other Short Stories

Preface

How Colors Came Into The World

"Once all the colors that existed were black and white. Then one day a space explorer (up in space) saw a mass of something. He didn't think the something had a name, so he named the something colors. They were very pretty. He grabbed the colors and took them back to Earth. Then everyone saw them. However a little boy named Sam broke the web that held the colors together. So all the colors went all over and stained everything. That is how colors came into the world. THE END."

—Pia Orleane, *seven years old*

When I was a child, I wrote the above story. That was before I realized the truth, or probably more accurately, before I could *explain* the truth. Yet somehow I *knew*. I was very young, and this was my first story. I was going to tell the world the truth!

As I grew up, I continued to write, but I stopped writing stories... until now. I wrote things that had a *scientific* background, things that could be researched. And then Cullen and I met Laarkmaa, the Pleiadian friends who always appear to Cullen and me as beautiful blue waves of energy. Their wisdom about how to use the energy of colors (shared in *Remembering Who We Are*[1]) gave me goosebumps. I have always chosen the color of my clothes each day based upon the energy I felt was present at the moment. As I flip through my closet, I feel the energy of each color and ask myself which color works best with the energy of the day? The colors always respond in their way, and their guidance has never let me down. I don't tell other people what I do when I choose my clothes for the day, but I often notice that many women choose to wear the same color as I do on a particular day. Something inside them remembers, even if they

---

[1] Orleane, P. and Smith, C. *Remembering Who We Are—Laarkmaa's Guidance on Healing the Human Condition*. 2015. Santa Fe, NM: One Water Press

don't consciously realize it. Colors have energy, vibration, and *meaning*. A wise person can use colors to bring more balance and flow into the day.

When I was 52, I died. That's not so unusual. People die all the time. But it was slightly unusual that this was the *second* time I had been declared legally dead, only to come back to life many, many days later. That's another story, but what is important here is that I came back to life with even more wisdom about the importance of colors! I saw rainbows of colors when I died. In fact, my entire body was made of rainbows—lovely waves of red, yellow, blue, green, pink, and violet. Could it be that as a child I remembered how colors were part of me? That we are supposed to use the gift of colors the space explorer of my childhood story brought to Earth to explore and better understand energy and how to work with it for more harmony?

Now I realize more deeply the magic of colors! I know because I experienced being all colors as they existed in me like a rainbow. In fact, I was completely in Rainbow body[2] before I returned to my current

---

[2] Our Pleiadian friends, Laarkmaa, have described the Rainbow body as the merging of our etheric body (or light body) with the physical body, creating a lighter body that consists of all the colors in the rainbow. We attain the ability to merge and create a Rainbow body through making conscious higher choices and eating a diet based on the principles of *Ahimsa*.

form. My first journey out of the house after that experience of being "dead" for a *very* long time came through an intuitive knowing that I needed a scarf of rainbow colors to remind me of who I am and where I had been. I asked Cullen to drive me to a particular store that I felt would have just what I needed. Since I could hardly walk, he was hesitant, but he agreed. When he parked in front of the store, I immediately saw my scarf in the window! As he purchased it for me, he found out that it was a handmade, one-of-a-kind item. I believe it was made for me.

Since my initial exploration of colors in the world, I have learned to live my life through a continual practice of two important principles that bring a richness of color and energy into my life: *In Lak'ech* and *Ahimsa*. *In Lak'ech* simply means, "I am another yourself." In other words, I have learned to see the reflection of myself in the eyes of everyone else. I see *In Lak'ech* as the blue energy of trust, for it provides trust in ourselves, in others, and in the Universe. There are differences of gifts and talents, of course, but otherwise I am the same as everyone else. This is a genuine reflection of Unity Consciousness in the blue energy of *In Lak'ech*.

The second principle *Ahimsa,* simply means, "Do no harm." That includes not only my actions, but also my thoughts. I know that every thought I have radiates out to touch others, here on Earth and deeper into the Universe. If I wallow in worried or negative thoughts or beliefs, that negative energy is dispersed from me, harming everyone and everything else, for everything is connected. If I allow my heart to guide my thoughts through feelings of trust, acceptance, kindness, and compassion, every thought helps to create a better world and assists Earth in her ascension process to become a higher vibrational cosmic world. I see *Ahimsa* as gold, radiating the energy of grace all around when we practice it.

I wrote *How Colors Came into the World* as a seven year-old child; it was the best way that I could express what I remembered. Now I am an older and wiser woman, and I have spent a lifetime remembering how colors came into the world and seeing how they have been misused. They are not meant to be used to separate us, as people split into factions based on the color of their skin or a certain color of flag to separate one country from another. They are meant to provide richness and texture of different perspectives to our experience so that we may experience a rainbow of opportunities!

It has taken a lot of courage to maintain the magical state of colors I achieved when I died. Following two principles taught to me by the Pleiadians, I have slowly shed my density, raising my vibration to a frequency where the energy of each color can not only exist, but can also radiate out from me into the world. I don't fully succeed in this every day; I am still learning. But often I do. When I died, I was in waveform, free! I was the rainbow itself. Before long I will return to that rainbow state again—for good.

The stories in this book are different colors of perspective, and each one holds a ticket to freedom. I hope they brighten your life and bring you closer to becoming a rainbow yourself!

Automated

Zachary jerked awake as the alarm in his head began to buzz. He didn't like this latest installation into his body. The company needed him to be on time for work, but they didn't allow him or anyone else the freedom to be responsible for themselves. Everything was automated. Struggling to sit upright, he staggered out of bed to begin his morning toiletries. He stepped into the shower as hot water automatically began to pummel him before suddenly switching to cold water to be sure he was thoroughly awake. He had no choice; this was the program. Each shower was regulated; each person was only allowed a limited amount of recycled water for drinking or bathing. All laundry was sent out once a week to the machines that cleansed everything with ultraviolet waves of light, then pressed, folded, packaged, and returned it to him, clean and crisp. Deliveries to and from the laundry were also scheduled like clockwork; every Thursday soiled laundry was picked up and clean laundry was delivered. He had no choice in his clothes either, nor in the decor of his private space. Everything in his private cubicle was a dull grey, and the clothes he wore were the standard navy blue. The monotonous colors of grey and navy blue were ubiquitous. He found the company's lack of imagination stifling.

Thinking this kind of thought, however, was dangerous. It would trigger a shimmer in his autonomic nervous system, thereby signaling that he needed calming. Once that shimmer was picked up by the internal sensor that had been installed into his body, an automatic dose of Denzitol[1] would be pumped into his system to steady and calm him. He did not even have the freedom of his own thoughts, much less the liberty to express feelings about what he thought. Ever since the city governors had decided that for the sake of harmony, emotions and thoughts were public domain that needed supervision and guidance,

---

[1] Denzitol—calming, anti-anxiety

his freedom and everyone else's freedom had been surrendered. It had been such a subtle and insidious plan. First, the city governors had introduced new technology that made everyone's lives seem easier. Cell phones were immediately available that never left your hand because they generated instant connection with other people, and more importantly, instant replies to any question asked. Computers were provided that offered such speedy response that you never had to wait for an answer. Slyly, the city governors supplied the answers they wanted people to believe. And because everything seemed so easy, people had not questioned how their history began to change or who was rearranging the facts. They stopped thinking about anything important at all after a while. Bit by bit, people surrendered their own authority to the machines that were continually being upgraded and offered as humanity's best friend for the future. From there, it was only a small step to having the machines installed into human skin, and later into organs. Advertisements displayed all over the district showed smiling faces that had no troubles after they agreed to the installations. Medical offices proclaimed that the machine parts would prevent illness and keep you young forever. And if you were anxious or upset, the machines would automatically fix the situation with a "natural" substance that would make you instantly feel happy again. Because people had stopped asking questions, they simply accepted that this was true. Before long, the schools and workplaces refused to accept anyone who did not have the newest technology installed into them. Of course, nobody wanted to be excluded from receiving the best education or getting the best job. And everyone believed that their total health depended upon the machines the doctors had installed into their systems.

Zachary barely remembered the last day he had been himself. He had struggled when they wanted to insert the implant, but his mother had held him firmly and allowed the doctors to make the incision. It was done without his having any voice at all in the situation, and when he cried, whatever they put inside of him took away his tears. Even his feelings were no longer his own. Later, more and more implants had been imposed on him, and as he adjusted to each one, he became more awkward and less fluid in both his movements and his thoughts. Zachary, like everyone else, became automated. With so many parts of himself mechanized, he questioned why he was still able to remember how it was before. He could not afford to think about it for long, however, or the sensor would dose him with Denzitol. Sometimes he could trick the system by meditating for a brief period and then thinking whatever he wanted. He had managed to do this for up to fifteen minutes after a meditation session before the sensor realized he had gone offline. But he couldn't take the time to do that now because he was expected at work.

After dressing in his required navy garb, he donned his visor and switched on the screen. Quickly scanning the numbers for the day he found the code that assigned his particular duties. There was not much variety in his job, but he did have the occasional deviation when someone else was being monitored by the company. Because of his advanced automation, Zachary was always the first line of investigation into anomalies others in the system expressed. He guessed he could be considered a spy. He sighed and then corrected himself before the internal monitor could pick up his irritation. He was sick and tired of being the eyes of the company, but he didn't have any choice. His job had been assigned when he was only five, and the city governors had discovered his mathematical skills and dexterity. Unlike many of the others, he was somewhat adroit at maneuvering the mechanical attachments that had become a part of him, while simultaneously filtering the company's ongoing drone of mechanical and electrical surveillance noises.

Because he was smart, he also knew how to divert the attention of the company when he wanted time alone. He didn't do it often because he did not want to create a pattern that would be noticed and investigated. But on days like this, when he was being assigned surveillance of another employee, it was easy to trick the company into believing he was doing his job as he slipped away into the only bit of Nature that still remained in the district. He loved to go into the small forest that had been saved to make it appear that the city governors cared for the planet. Most of it was artificial, of course, but there were real trees, and there was a small artificial creek that had been dug into the ground where machines pumped some of the precious recycled water in a short cycle from the top of the creek to the bottom and back again. No one ever asked why the creek suddenly started and then just as suddenly stopped rather than flowing naturally through the forest. They didn't remember how a creek in Nature really flowed. Zachary had to be careful here. If he raised his endorphins too much through enjoying this small Nature experience, he would trigger another one of the technical monitors in his brain, and he would be given a dose of Klamedin[2]. He hated this one most of all, for it dulled his thinking, and he felt like he was stuck in tar. But he managed to keep his neurological system within the prescribed ranges by only allowing very limited moments of real feelings or important thoughts.

Zachary felt his artificial attachments most when he was in this forest. He felt stiff, awkward, and he was aware that he moved more like a machine than like he had moved as a boy, when he could run or stop as he chose. He clinked and jerked with every step now, since his brain was no longer in charge of his movements. The implant at the base of his skull dictated his rhythm and his speed. He could program *where* he was going, but

---

[2] Klamedin—dulls thinking

not *how.* Jerking down the path, step by clumsy step, he made his way between the trees to the beginning of the simulated creek and slowly bent to position himself on the ground. It was awkward, but he managed to jerk himself down and quiet all the sensors that were not accustomed to this position. For the moment he was safe from the sensors, undetected in this unusual posture. He regulated his breath and adjusted the visor to indicate that he was following the assignment. He would figure out how to add this into the report later. For now, he just wanted to be in this place and imagine that once again, he was part of Nature, too.

And then he saw her. At first it was just a flash of movement through the trees. He thought the sun and shadow were playing tricks on his eyes. He blinked and then kept looking, noticing that his breathing was quickening and his heart rate was speeding up. Quickly, to avoid a drug dosage, he input a status report that he was following the suspect at a hurried pace. Then he looked where the girl had appeared and saw her again, this time more clearly. She peeked out from behind one of the trees, shy and curious. Zachary was a bit unwieldy as he struggled to his feet, but he was compelled to do so. His quiet moment was over, and now his entire attention was riveted on something he was having a hard time believing. The girl moved from behind the tree, taking a few tentative steps toward him. He stood expression-less, watching her to see what she would do next. Where did she come from? He knew everybody in the district, or so he believed. She was definitely not from here. She was dressed in a soft yellow garment that followed the curves of her body. She cocked her head and cautiously moved to where he was standing, absolutely flowing with every step she took. She appeared to have no metal or technical parts directing her feet or her hands or anything about her. Zachary could hardly believe it! Before he knew it, she had reached him and was touching the lump on his temple, where his latest implant had been installed, the one that now awakened him every morning. Slowly her fingers traveled over the lumpy flesh of the raised scar and the hard material beneath it. She looked up into his eyes and asked, "Why?"

Because Zachary had no answer for that ques-tion, he said nothing. He just stood there, doing his best to regulate his quickening rhythms. She touched her heart and said, "Jasmine." Touching his lips, she then asked, "Who?"

He almost choked as he spit out his name, harsher than he had intended. She pulled back, startled, but she did not run away. Following her lead, he touched his own heart and answered again, more softly this time, "Zachary."

Again he wondered where she came from. How was it that she seemed to have no implants, no technical parts, and she could move so freely? Monitoring his own technology was a full time job, and he could not imagine how she had managed to free herself from the installation of the implants. How had she gone to school? Where did she work? How did she live? If he weren't on this special assignment today, he was certain he would have been dosed by now, for his brain was firing question after question and his heart was racing. Now adopting her own form of single word speech, he asked her, "Where?"

She turned her head toward the trees where he had first seen her, and just shrugged. Then slowly she turned back around, leaned over the creek, and dangled her fingers into the water. After a moment, she suddenly stood up and started to move back across the path to the trees. But after only a few steps she stopped again just as suddenly, and said, "Again." And then she vanished through the trees as quickly as she had appeared. The only thing Zachary could do was to regulate his own rhythms and store this experience to think about after a meditation session. He needed to return to work and file his report. The day was coming to a close, and his superior would want an account immediately. Suspicious company members had to be dealt with.

Back at the office, the steady eyes of his supervisor glared at him across the desk, waiting. Zachary had had to fabricate a story about Timothy Roberts, the suspect, something that was plausible but potentially harmless to Timothy, who Zachary actually knew nothing about. He had only seen Timothy in passing, just enough to remember what he looked like. However, Zachary had learned first-hand what power the company had over a human when as a teenager, he had tried to run away from the additional intrusive procedures they had inflicted upon him. The lights posted all around the city reflected signals from satellites that sent painful irradiating energy in direct beams to troublemakers or to those who were resistant. All the company or the city governors had to do was enter your particular data, which they owned from years of collecting information from people's Internet and Facebook use, and the excruciating beams of irradiating energy shot into your field, stopping you in your tracks as you collapsed in pain and unbearable heat. He would not do that to Timothy or anyone else. As he monitored his words and breath so as not to trigger any abnormal responses in his system, he told his supervisor, who was the company manager, of following Timothy into the forest where he stood for awhile before returning to the company. There was nothing else to report. The man, however, was not satisfied and continued to glare at Zachary. He wanted more. He wanted the surveillance to reveal a pattern that could be dealt with. Zachary was certain from his supervisor's greedy look, that tomorrow his assignment would be similar to today's, but, of course, it was never disclosed until the numbers in his visor revealed the code of the assignment. That's the way it worked. He prepared to leave but was surprised by an offhand comment the company manager let slip. Something about suspecting Timothy had been frequenting the forbidden zone beyond the forest. Zachary hadn't even known there was a forbidden zone, for his automation did not allow him to wander too far from his prescribed areas of work and home. He stored the comment away to think about after a meditation, when it would not be detected.

The next morning, as he had expected, the code in his visor again assigned his surveillance of Timothy, but with the additional numbers indicating that he was to focus on going directly to the forest and watch for Timothy's arrival and departure. He was to follow him. This was an unexpected gift. He could do his job and simultaneously watch to see if Jasmine returned. He waited throughout the morning near the creek, staring into the trees, but no one appeared and nothing happened. Then, as the sun moved from morning into the early afternoon sky, she stepped out of the trees and came towards him. This time he allowed the muscles of his face to move into a position he remembered from childhood. It was called a smile, and although it looked somewhat artificial on his mechanically controlled features, his eyes showed her that it was genuine. He was glad to see her. Today she seemed to recognize that their time was limited and that there was danger around him. Using her simple one word at a time vocabulary she took his hand and said, "Freedom."

Intrigued, yet wondering what she could possibly mean, he quickly replied, "When?" adjusting his internal monitors to keep his systems within the standard acceptable range.

"Tomorrow," she said, touching his hand. "Here."

Zachary was confused by this. The forest was small, and just the two of them were present, but he knew that the company sensors could penetrate any part of the district, or the whole world as far as he knew, if they chose. How could she possibly offer him freedom? He knew that he was powerless to escape them; he had tried.

Seeing his puzzled look, she again moved to touch his face and then his heart. "Trust," she said, and then she turned to go. Zachary could do nothing but wait until the day was over and then walk in his lurching, artificial pace back to the company office to report that he had not yet connected with Timothy. He needed to buy more time. He needed to steal a few minutes after work to meditate so that he could have the liberty to think about what was happening for his stolen fifteen minutes.

When he had his fifteen minutes, his thoughts filled with questions and then more questions. None of them seemed possible to resolve. Going into the sleep realm at the appointed time that night proved difficult, but he regulated his breathing and heart rate enough to prevent a dose of Zorophin[3]. He did not want to feel drugged in the morning. It was potentially an important day, and he wanted to be completely clear.

On the third morning, he found he had secured the additional time he needed in the forest. Extra codes had been added to his visor, instructing him to accost Timothy and use electrical force to bring him back to the company. He didn't even know where Timothy was, but he took a chance on satisfying the company supervisor by continuing this false search and creating a plausible story that would save Timothy from whatever penalty the company planned for his diversion and absence. At the end of the day, he planned to send a message that he had found Timothy collapsed in a state

---

[3] Zorophin—sleep inducing

of overdose because one of his sensors had over-reacted, causing a triple release of Denzitol. This in turn caused an adverse reaction of panic, which his internal system then treated by delivering a double dose of Klamedin. Zachary would explain that he had found Timothy completely immobilized, unable to think or to move. He would further report that he had taken him to an outlying medical facility to have his sensors adjusted and the antidote given for the overdose. The story would buy Zachary more time and temporarily save Timothy, but the company would figure it out soon enough. He only hoped Timothy had indeed somehow magically escaped.

Now having reached the forest, Zachary turned his attention away from his plan and looked towards the trees, hoping to see Jasmine. He was pleased that she appeared earlier this morning than he had anticipated, and this time she was not alone. There was another who moved quickly and fluidly like she did with her. He stiffened, in an automatic response to possible danger, but quickly realized that he was reacting inappropriately to the situation, so he relaxed and jerked his way closer to where they stood at the edge of the trees.

Jasmine said, "Quickly," taking his hand. He really liked the way he felt when she touched him, but he had to work exceptionally hard to balance his system when it happened. He didn't want any unusual physical or emotional reactions to register on the sensors, causing him to be dosed and re-regulated. He was fighting with all his strength to modulate his own body in this new experience. Suddenly her companion pushed him very hard into a tree. He expected pain, but found there was no impact with the tree, and therefore no pain. In fact, the tree held a portal that he passed through, with Jasmine now ahead of him and her companion behind him. They were taking him somewhere he had not known existed. The shock and surprise immediately caused a dose of Denzitol to be released, calming his body, but confusing his mind. He saw swirls of color all around him, felt himself move as if he were floating, and then suddenly he was in a different world. The sunshine was bright. There was running water nearby; it sounded wilder than the artificial creek he was accustomed to hearing. This water had a flow of its own. Jasmine was holding his hand, looking carefully at his face. Her companion had disappeared, but now in his place was another, an older man with white hair and wrinkles on his face. In his dazed state Zachary somehow registered that these people did not have any technological devices implanted or attached to them. They walked with ease and flow. They spoke little, but communicated through looks, touch, and single words. He liked it. He felt strangely safe and alive.

Jasmine put her hand on the older man's heart, looking at Zachary, and said, "Father." She followed this message by pointing to something the older man held in his hand and said, "Help" pointing next to Zachary. Now she touched his heart and said, "Trust."

Zachary's confusion increased as his internal dosing mechanism now released a heavy dose of Klamedin, pushing his body into a state of immobility. As he looked from Jasmine to her father, he somehow accepted that they were going to help him. Then everything became a blur.

When Zachary next became aware, he felt a slight pain in his head. Without opening his eyes, he reached up to touch the lump where his latest installation had occurred. It was gone. There was no lump. There was no hard material in his temple. It was simply sore. Now he opened his eyes. There were people stirring around him, but no one was watching him. He slowly registered that he was in a community of some sort. But these people were very different from the people to which he was accustomed. These people were moving about freely. They were laughing. Some of them were producing musical sounds from their mouths. It was astounding! He saw Jasmine turn from the group, somehow aware that he had awakened. She picked up a pile of old wires and computer hardware and walked over to where he lay. "Finished," she said, pointing to the pile of garbled wires and bits and pieces and then pointing to Zachary, "Free."

Expecting the usual dose when he thought too much or too freely, Zachary was cautious as he took in what she was explaining. But nothing happened. His body felt different. He tested his reactions, questioning, "How?" He experienced no panic. No anxiety. Just curiosity and interest. And a new sensation: Hope! It seemed he really was free. Again he asked, "How?"

Jasmine reached to touch him, moving her hands from the top of his head to his stomach. She said, "Truth."

Zachary was confused, and Jasmine saw he needed more understanding. She touched his body again and said, "Truth." After a slight pause, she followed that thought with "Here" as she touched his body once again, this time on his heart.

Something clicked inside of him. Memories of childhood came flooding back into Zachary, helping him adjust to his new freedom. He looked around the small group of people and saw that each one was moving freely around the area, without the artificial jerks caused by the sensor implants. No one had the drugged expression he was so accustomed to seeing. And no one had the hard mechanical glare the company directors and city governors had either. With Jasmine's help, he had truly escaped. A bit farther from him he saw Timothy Roberts. He registered surprise, followed by the instant awareness that he had, in his own way, also helped Timothy to escape by not trying to find him or investigate where he had gone. There did not appear to be any technology of any kind here, not even the lights that reflected satellite signals that controlled everyone. He did not know where he had gone, but he realized that this small group of people was not being affected or controlled by technology here. This group was demonstrating the possibility that humanity could be saved from further intervention of Artificial Intelligence by the way that they lived. Maybe humans would once again be free to make their own choices and live sharing their own thoughts and feelings. Jasmine seemed to instinctively know what he was thinking. She smiled and pointing first to her head and then to his own, she said, "Shared." Then she smiled again and pointed first to her heart and then to his and said again, "Shared." He gradually comprehended what she was saying. He realized that she was telling him that his thoughts and feelings affected everyone else, because here everyone shared what they thought and what they felt; thoughts and feelings were not controlled artificially. It allowed for a transparent way of living with intuitive communication. He liked it. People smiled. They helped each other. And now he was going to be one of them.

He tried to stand up but found he was very weak and unbalanced. Jasmine smiled and said, "Rest." Again he knew what she meant. It was going to take time for his body to adjust to functioning under his own commands and natural rhythms. The sensors, the stores of drugs and injectors had been removed, but there were still residual effects of both the intrusive technological implants and the aftermath of continual dosing. Still, unlike most, he had always maintained some sense of mind and body control through his practice of meditation. He knew that he would adjust soon enough and that he would be able to walk like these people did, with ease and flow. He would be able to think whatever he wanted, knowing that each thought was shared with his new community. He could feel his own feelings, which also radiated out into the community. Instantly he understood that now that he had been liberated, he was responsible for keeping his own thoughts and feelings away from anxiety, fear, judgment, or blame, for those kinds of thoughts and feelings were harmful to everyone. He was responsible for developing and increasing feelings of trust, gratitude, patience, kindness, and compassion. And something else was stirring within him—a new feeling. He looked up at Jasmine with a question?

She smiled and said, "Love."

Zachary was finally free. He was experiencing life as it was intended to be. He was appreciative, and he knew he would work to help these people protect the zone where they lived free from the technical world. He did not know what dimension or zone he had crossed when he came through the portal in the tree, but every moment he felt more grateful for this magnificent change in his life. Another feeling was coming into him.

Again, through her intuitive knowing, Jasmine read his feelings and responded, "Joy!"

Yes, Zachary thought. She was right; this new feeling was the joy of being free.

Angel in the Trenches

Preta didn't talk about her life—not because she lacked experiences or was ashamed of what she had lived, but because she was not interested. It bored her. She had never liked history because it was a collection of old, tired, dead stories. Her history was not different. It could have been any-body's story. Stories were always full of pain and either personal progress or pictures of where one was stuck, and she had long ago decided that it didn't matter what shaped the story; pain was pain. The need for people to tell their stories was based on a need to be seen and recognized for whom they believed themselves to be. Most people's stories were based on experiences of separation, full of walls of fear being built around their hearts, fear of being annihilated from a lack of love. Long ago she had learned that the attachment to one's personal story and the need for validation kept people locked into patterns that furthered their sense of separation. She was not interested in that. She was interested in unity, and thus had adopted the stance that we are all the same, and our personal stories are irrelevant. One's power grew by turning towards the divine spark that connected to others in unity, not through attachment to stories they believed defined them. At least that is how she viewed her life at work as a certified counselor.

But knowing these things did not stop the drama from unfolding around her in her personal life. She struggled as much as all of the people she counseled, maybe even more so, when she allowed herself to think about her life, which was not often. Although she refused to dwell on her past, new and different experiences that added more pain continually arose for Preta. She learned that if she focused on her pain, she found herself judging both herself and others, and she got stuck. If she focused on whatever pleasure she might experience, she was just as stuck, bound by the desire to have more pleasure or to avoid further pain. The only way through life was to simply accept what came, without attachment. She knew that. Somewhere inside her lived another part of herself that continually reminded her that this was just a play, so she needed to play her part well.

Every day Preta listened to stories as people complained about their lives or tried to improve upon their partners. They did very little to change their own lives because they expected her to listen to their stories and fix their problems. She heard constant grumbling and criticism, as a wife or husband whined about little insignificant differences. As their stories unfolded she heard their pain and witnessed the "victim status" they so eagerly embraced from years of feeling judged or blamed. Sometimes she drifted off, momentarily reflecting on the same patterns in her own life, but not often. She didn't like to look back. When she did, she had the general sense of everyone always wanting to improve upon her, a theme filled with comments that used to pierce her heart before she learned to simply brush them aside as irrelevant.

"Don't walk like that."

"Don't move around so much—Be still."

"Don't show your teeth when you smile."

"Don't be so changeable. Make up your mind."

"Don't...don't...don't...*don't*"

People were always trying to fit her into a box of some kind that matched their own expectations. The funny thing was that the things that they tried to correct were her natural and positive responses to life. She *liked* the way she walked quietly, so that no one could hear her. It allowed her to be in the woods with the creatures she loved. She could be still then, because she was in harmony with the rhythms of the forest. She *liked* her warm smile, for it came right from her heart. And how could she *not* be changeable when circumstances were always changing around her? She had learned early on that others did not easily tolerate her genuine happiness, and so she lost her happy appearance. Other people always wanted to keep her in a box where they could predict what she would do. She had tried to fit in. She had tried to shrink into the tiny life that they were demanding of her, but her heart would never let her. As she had tried desperately to meet others' expectations, she sometimes asked herself questions such as,

"How can you direct a sunbeam where or how to shine?"

"How can you tell a star that its twinkle is not right?"

"How can you tell an angel that her perspective is wrong?"

But if she were a sunbeam or a star or an angel, she thought she surely would make people happier. Her natural joy kept leaking out into the world, until finally the weight of others' expectations forced her to adopt the view that everything was just a story, and all stories were alike—full of pain and the need to get beyond it. She stopped smiling so much. She became even more quiet. And she trained and became a counselor.

Although Preta's own life was full of challenges and problems she had not yet resolved, she genuinely worked to help others sort out their own lives. Every day she rode her bicycle fifteen minutes up a series of small hills to the center where she worked as a counselor for the homeless, the abused, those going through divorce, those who had lost a child, or those who were suffering in some way that was too large for them to manage. The world was full of pain, and she saw her job as helping to lift some of the burden from shoulders that were severely bent from too heavy a load. She listened. She talked. She held them as they cried. Sometimes she sang. There were many who shared her story of having been judged, pushed, shoved, or forced into tiny lives. Sometimes she privately questioned what she and they were doing here on Earth? She saw that each person has his or her own beauty and path of learning. No matter how different their stories, they were all struggling to find assurance, comfort, and happiness. They wanted to be loved.

Of course, there was little she could do to alleviate their circumstances, but Preta could help them see past the pain as they told their stories. She worked tirelessly, listening to their stories and offering her counsel. So many stories—all full of pain. At the end of the day, she freed herself of these stories as she rode home on her bicycle, her hair streaming in the wind as she pedaled as hard as she could before she coasted down the longest hill to her house and garden. It was the first of her daily rituals to release what was not hers and to reclaim herself. The second ritual was a long, hot bath. And then, after a cup of tea, she would go outside to visit her garden.

The garden was her special domain, the one place where she felt happy. She loved every plant in that garden, and she knew each one intimately

—who needed the shade of the big tree and who loved the sun, who preferred to wait for the rain to drink and who had an unquenchable thirst that required her watering. She cared for all their needs, tenderly clearing their leaves from the occasional bugs or debris, watching over them with all her gentle awareness. There were brilliant colors in all directions, flowers of all shapes and smells, brightly colored peppers and lettuce, marigolds that kept most of the bugs away. There was no obvious order to how she planted things, and to a casual observer, it might seem chaotic. But everything was indeed in an order of sorts, for she planted by her intuition, knowing exactly where each plant needed to be to get what it needed. Her garden had feminine curves and surprises everywhere you looked. She loved breathing in the smells of the rich, dark, moist earth combined with the sweet and astringent scents of flowers, herbs, and vegetables. Everything was perfect. This was her world.

There was Russian sage standing guard at the edges of the garden, waving royal colors of greeting. Her eyes slowly moved across the expanse of shapes and colors. The lilies drew her eyes first with their pink, white, yellow, and orange throats open to the sun, but then the bright, simple faces of the daisies smiled up to greet her. The yellows and pinks and purples of gladiolas and hollyhock beside the blue delphinium were so lively as they moved back and forth in a sea of hope and cheer. The purity and sweetness of the jasmine, whose fragrance fed the soul, and the silken petals of the roses in softest yellow, brilliant coral, red, and pink in various stages from bud to bloom offered inspiration as she gazed at their beauty and absorbed their sweet bouquet. And she could not forget the strong, little lavender, who did its best to always calm her. Here and there between the flowers was an occasional head of lettuce or broccoli or a bright red pepper plant. Aloe, lemon thyme, basil, and rosemary mingled in between, bringing hints of balance and healing. Across the path from the garden, next to the house, azaleas, rhododendron, and laurel shared their profuse blooms in varying hues of pink, white, red, and purple, while soft grasses along the path waved a welcome as if they were actually inviting her to step into her magical kingdom. All of her creative energies went into her garden, and it thrilled her every time a new green sprout peeked out of the ground, reaching for the sun. Large, round rocks offered places to rest, and a huge oak tree gave its shade. These rocks, the tree, and the plants were her friends, offering beauty, fragrance, healing, comfort, and joy to Preta.

Today after her bath, Preta wrapped the soft large towel around her and peered into the mirror, asking herself, "Who am I really?" It was a common question for her, but one to which she had not yet found an answer. Her ancestors had given her the dark skin of ancient Persia, which caused her to stand out against a background of people of lighter skin. Preta was pretty in an unusual way. She was short and curvy, with the kind of figure that made men turn to stare. One of her friends called her arresting. Her dark, wavy hair cascaded down her back, normally. Now she had it pinned up from her bath. Staring into the mirror, her large black eyes stared back, unblinking, full of life, but subdued and ready for the promise of something better.

As she dressed in her jeans and T-shirt and made her way into the living room, her thoughts turned to Damien, the child she had lost. He had been beautiful, tiny, with little blonde curls beginning to show on his innocent young head. He had his father's light hair and her dark skin and eyes, an interesting and unusual combination. Small and fragile, Damien had struggled to be here, gasping for breath in his sleep, until one night his tiny light went out as he drifted back to wherever he had come from. She knew in her heart that he simply had not found enough love to keep him here, although she had given him all she had. The world was too hard. When he died, her heart had broken, little pieces of hope falling around her feet. Preta had felt her own breathing would stop, too, the morning she picked up his small lifeless form and held it to her. Silent tears streamed down her face, her body racking with quiet sobs. Damien's father was glad enough for the burden to be gone. He merely shrugged as he looked at the dead child and its mother in tears, telling her to get over it. That day Preta had left him, looking for a bigger heart.

Her previous marriage and her work with others in her therapy practice gave her insights to help people in pain. However, even as a therapist who had been through a bad marriage, she still had managed to make another poor choice in her next marriage. With a sigh, she sank into the couch, deciding to calm her thoughts before going into her beloved garden. For six years now she had been with Gregory. Too late and in spite of her clinical training, Preta discovered that she had been fooled by and married a narcissist. He was not a cruel man, like Damien's father had been, but neither did he value her in the way he should. Mostly he was so self-indulgent that he barely noticed her unless he wanted something. He prided himself on how smart he was, how good he looked, and on how much influence he had over others, which was certainly less than he desired. Gregory had been drawn to Preta's unusual beauty and wanted her as a trophy he could display, another symbol of his success. She had accepted his pursuit of her, without knowing why. There was really nothing that drew them together. He was restless and bored, never satisfied with anything because he was never satisfied with himself. Before Preta, he was constantly moving from house to house, each one bigger than the last. When he met her, she had convinced him that his present home—soon to be hers—was just right. As soon as she moved in, she set to work planting her garden.

She was about to go outside when the front door slammed, taking her from her thoughts and back to reality as Gregory banged through the door. He was not a quiet person, like she was. She was silent, soundlessly moving from one place to the next. Like a cat, no one ever heard her because her step was light in the world. Gregory made himself known wherever he went, always hoping to be noticed. She opened her mouth to say hello, but he was already complaining loudly about his son-of-a-bitch manager before even removing his sports jacket. It was his first ritual upon arriving. He never asked about her day or how she was because his total focus was on himself. He was completely narcissistic. She listened vaguely to the usual assortment of complaints, thinking how each grievance had the same theme: he was a victim. But beneath today's rant was an undercurrent of something different she couldn't understand. It felt undefined, but dangerous. His tirade continued as he stamped into the kitchen, looking for a beer, the second of his coming home rituals. She didn't need alcohol, for she tried to meet whatever came to her directly, but Gregory believed a couple of beers "helped him to unwind." Watching from where she sat, she knew it was going to be more than a couple of beers tonight, and he was more likely to be riled than soothed by his drinking.

Preta didn't bother to get up now because there was no reason to do so. She leaned over from her cross-legged position on the couch, put down her now empty cup, and picked up a magazine, aimlessly flipping through it. The late afternoon sun streamed through a window, casting an angelic radiance around her. Breathing slowly, she softly toned under her breath, her own calming ritual, used whenever she sensed a storm. With beer in hand, Gregory came and stood over her, as if he wanted something, but not saying what it was he wanted. His face was scrunched into an unpleasant scowl, and his breathing was a bit erratic. Holding her own breath, she stopped toning and looked up questioning, but he just glared, his unhappiness seeping out of him and over her like a cloud of suffocating dust filling the air. Glancing down at the floor, she noticed he was standing on top of one of her delicate slippers, a subtle unconscious statement that screamed that he was the dominant one in the family and that she did not matter. The fact that he didn't even consider not putting his disgustingly dirty shoes worn into the city on top of the lovely slippers that she slid onto her clean feet after a bath spelled out just exactly how little he thought of her. She sighed, realizing she shouldn't focus on the hundreds of pictures that illustrated her life as they registered in her consciousness. She knew they were symbols spelling out the meaning in her choices, but she remained frozen by an inexplicable inability to make necessary changes in her own life.

Suddenly Gregory turned and stamped off towards the screen door off the kitchen, carelessly sloshing his beer with every step. He was going into her garden. Without thinking, she automatically sprang up to go after him.

The brilliant rainbow of colors and the sweet floral and damp earthy smells called Preta, as always. But this evening was different. In the middle of all this beauty, something was out of balance. Even her plants sensed it, and she could see some of the blossoms closing for the night much earlier than they should in the late afternoon sun. Although she could not identify what was wrong, Petra knew that it was coming from Gregory. She walked over to him, consciously taking his hand and asking if he would like to go out to dinner. He jerked his hand away, trembling with an unspoken rage. Puzzled, she stepped back and watched. He had been angry often enough, but she had never seen him like this. She could not imagine what had happened, for although he always talked about himself, he never really told her anything of importance. The presence of fear began to climb up her neck in little prickles, and she sensed real and inexplicable danger. It was palpable now, more than the niggling feeling in her stomach she had first felt.

Unknown to her because he never shared anything that mattered with Preta, Gregory had lost his job in a most embarrassing way today. Having fought his way to a senior position in the investment firm where he worked, and believing himself to be smarter than anyone else at the company, he had made a severe misjudgment in his choice of handling their largest client's funds. He had borrowed from his client's account, thinking that he could quickly repay it without discovery from the interest of an illegal investment he made off the record. But the company in which he had invested had been headlined in today's papers, claiming bankruptcy to avoid governmental charges for illegal activities. And he had been part of that. Under government pressure, all investors in the company had been publically named, including Gregory. Simultaneously, in a sweep of karma landing squarely in his face, the firm's largest client had arrived at his office this morning wishing to withdraw a substantial amount from her portfolio for a long European tour she planned to enjoy with her granddaughter, who was graduating from university. The funds were not there, and in the light of the unfolding truth, Gregory's illusion of his own brilliance and power had died. He lost his job, his self-respect, and his idea of who he was. That had been his first big mistake.

His second mistake was to kick the dirt in Preta's garden, uprooting one of the peppers and bruising a nearby delphinium. This is where the story took a sudden turn, hurtling them both towards an unhappy ending. Preta gasped and automatically lunged for Gregory, pushing him with all her strength away from her precious plants. In a flash containing all her own unresolved grief, she pushed with all her might to stop him from harming anything in her garden, some part of her connecting the fact that while she had not been able to save her small son, she could save these helpless, little, living plants. All of her energy went into stopping an attack on her plants. Without words, the rest unfolded in gasping breaths and startled reflexes. In a single moment Gregory, who was much larger than Preta, released his anger and his shame in a violent swing that caught Preta in the chest taking her breath and causing her to lose her balance. She stumbled toward him in a blind fall. Falsely believing that she was going to attack him, he struck her again. This time the blow landed squarely on her brow, spinning her around so that she fell backwards, her head crashing onto a rock at the edge of the garden. Dazed and breathless, Preta silently asked for help.

The next thing she knew she was floating, looking down at her body in the garden. There was a pool of bright crimson flowing from her head onto her beloved plants. Gregory was standing over her, stunned, unable to take in what had happened. She didn't feel any pain, but she could see the gaping wound on her head, where it had cracked open on the rock. Her rock. She had stood there often while watering her garden.

Slowly Preta's sight began to shift, and her focus turned to the lovely tones and singing around her. She continued to float, slowly drifting away from the scene below. Gregory seemed to be shrinking, but it was actually she who was moving farther and farther away. She felt, rather than saw, her plants thanking her and waving goodbye. Someone had taken her by the hand and was leading her away. At least it felt like touch, but she realized that she had no body to touch now. Mysteriously she felt the comfort of that imagined touch as if it were real. Then she realized that it was real. It was energy. An energetic being of light was beside her, reflecting the energy of light into to her. As she looked, she could see that she herself was now made of waves of energy, and she was spilling light all around her. She suddenly felt a familiar presence—angels, or what she had always believed were angels. They had appeared often enough in her dreams in their light-filled forms, comforting her or teaching her how to fly. Now they were lifting her pain, as she had tried to lift all those souls she had touched at work when she listened to their sad stories. She remembered all the stories. So many of them, and her job had been to carry them all, to bring comfort where she could, and to try her best to ease their pain. Instinctively she knew that she really had been an angel in the trenches, helping to lift their pain. Suddenly she understood that she had been living a story, too. Her own story was over now.

The angels around her showed her how she had avoided her own inner work while focusing on helping others. Wordlessly they showed her how she had often not made good choices for herself, and that her story could have been different if she had. She accepted this as truth, knowing that she had learned her lessons, and it no longer mattered. She felt neither pain nor pleasure, only the simple essence of being. And most of all, she felt what she had always longed for. She felt loved. She was no longer in the trenches. At last this angel had found the unity she had been seeking. Finally she was going home.

Weaving Light

Mary was about as inconspicuous as anyone I had ever seen. She had a thin frame of a body, almost slight enough that a wisp of wind could carry her away. Her small face was framed by mousy brown hair that hung to the bottom of her chin, where it was cut into a straight line. Her eyes were hazel, and her mouth was a thin line that changed her face when she smiled. She lived alone, working to repair clothing, draperies, or any material that needed patching or repair. No one in the community seemed to know where she came from, and few had any interest in her, except for the tasks she performed without complaint. When I accidentally knocked on her door, thinking it was the address of someone else, she offered me a cup of herbal tea. In that moment I began a tentative friendship with her because she seemed lonely. And so was I. With no family and few friends, I felt very alone in the world. No one seemed to understand me or share my interests in making the world a better place. People always came to me with their stories, and I listened, but after telling their story, they would go right back to the same situation without making any changes. Little challenges in jobs or relationships passed after whatever drama they chose to engage, and life went on, unchanged. So what good was the patience I practiced in listening quietly to them? What good were the comments I made to help them? I wanted to make a difference. I wanted to change the poverty, the discord, the disconnection I witnessed every day. Everyone else around me seemed not to care. As long as they had their coffee and their cell phones, they were content. As I looked at the people I passed every day, I felt like I was from another planet. What was I doing here?

I began my friendship with Mary cautiously, not knowing what to expect. I had opened myself in friendship to so many, only to be lied to, cheated, or unexpectedly betrayed. It wasn't that I no longer trusted people; I just wanted them to show me who they were before I gave them my whole heart. Mary seemed to understand my caution. From the first moment we met, she began to help me to understand exactly who she was. Much of it was without words. Her gentle nature, the tone of her voice, her letting me sit quietly and watch as she worked demonstrated a simple kind of trust that grew between us. She never told me where she was from, but I didn't care. I seemed to have more in common with Mary than anyone I had ever met. When I dropped by her place after work or on the weekends, she always welcomed me with a cup of herbal tea and a smile. Often we sat in silence, watching the sun stream through the windows until it set in the early evening. I felt at peace with Mary.

Our friendship strengthened and deepened through both shared silence and genial conversations as the days passed. Mary seemed to understand my thoughts about the emotional disruptions that I experienced so constantly around me. It seemed everyone I met was always upset about something; they were either frustrated, angry, jealous, or sad, and freely discharging those emotions on everyone in their path. I actually felt physically sick when I was around too much of this negative energy, and I wished people would think about how their emotional outbursts and thoughtless remarks made an impact on others. But they didn't seem to notice or care. Everybody I knew seemed to believe they had the right to pollute the entire environment with their own messy, emotional states. I kept my feelings to myself, rarely letting anyone see me cry or get angry. I practiced patience with others, and yet, it seemed they rarely even noticed if something they said or did could be harmful to me. Mary said that she believed emotions were signals that we ourselves were out of balance and that they had very little to do with other people or outer circumstances. She felt that when others were emotional, it was a reflection of their own imbalances; otherwise, they would respond calmly and effectively to whatever was occurring, rather than reacting with explosive or inconsiderate words and actions.

"Emotions, if not properly used, can be dangerous for both the person feeling them and for those on whom they are projected," Mary said.

"Therefore," she continued, "it is each person's responsibility to think clearly about why they are being so emotionally affected."

She said that people would grow much more quickly into better versions of themselves if they would simply examine what they were thinking when they were upset and consider that there *could* be another way to see the situation. I knew she was right.

One day Mary began to speak about light and energy and how each one of us is made of these things. Instantly I resonated with what she was saying, and I knew this was true. We are far more than the form of our physical bodies. Something blazed inside of me when I listened to Mary speaking of these things; I had somehow always known they were true. To think of myself as light gave me a sense of purpose. Light shines. Maybe the purpose I had been seeking was about to be revealed through our friendship. She talked about changing forms as we integrated more and more light into who we are, calling the new form a Rainbow body.

"In this Rainbow body," Mary explained, "our etheric energetic self merges with our denser physical self, radiating all the colors and energies of the rainbow. The Rainbow body combination is less dense," she said, "and of a higher vibration."

Mary told me that to change into a Rainbow body form, we had to make many, many conscious choices, changing our belief systems, old patterns of reaction and behavior, and even our diet. I was fascinated as Mary shared these ideas with me. Everything made sense. I had been a vegetarian all of my life because of my conscious choice not to eat an animal whose life had been taken to support my own. That just felt wrong to me. Now with Mary's explanation of choosing the highest good for *everyone* and *everything*, my vegetarianism made even more sense. The evening after that particular shared conversation, I left Mary's presence feeling even lighter, happier, and more at peace than usual after our meetings.

The next day I learned that I would be required to work late. Most of the other men at my job had families, and it had become normal for them to push any extra work on me. Everyone assumed that I would not mind because I didn't have anyone at home waiting for me. I was a quiet man, living a quiet life, with no reason not to work late, they assumed. I sighed. I would not be able to go to Mary's that evening, which saddened me, but I quietly focused on all the things we had discussed as I worked to finish the task at hand. I knew that I had to keep this job to pay my bills, but I was beginning to realize that I also had another, even more important job. I had to keep making choices that were for the highest good for all, until others could see that there was another way to live other than through the competition and conflict that surrounded us all. It wasn't going to be easy, but then I had been challenged all of my life by being different. Now I would make my difference count.

The next time I was able to visit Mary, she was sitting at a loom that I had never noticed, having been hidden by a curtain behind her normal work station. She was weaving a new piece of fabric, something I had never seen before. It sparkled and shone with radiance like diamonds in the night sky. I knew that Mary was showing me her trust by allowing me to see this private work of art. She appeared to be a master weaver, her nimble fingers swiftly moving the shuttle back and forth between the warp and the woof of the cloth. There were dark knots in places, but as Mary continued weaving, they magically disappeared, dissolving into more pieces of light in the fabric. Something magical was happening, and I was certain that it was more than just creating a new piece of cloth.

As Mary continued weaving, she picked up bits and threads of our previous conversations over the weeks that had passed. Carefully, she began to explain the task of weaving this particular piece of cloth.

"This cloth is made of all the thoughts and feelings expressed by people collectively, which create your reality," she began. "When people cooperate and share their ideas together, the fabric of life is smooth and beautiful. The knots you see are the manifestation of all the unresolved emotions of jealousy, fear, anger, and sadness that create the competition, greed, separation, and suffering people experience. Most people cling to these knots, rather than trying to unwind and resolve them. The more knots, the more people collectively feel and believe the world is full of pain and distress instead of joy and connection. Each person needs to do his or her own work to unknot the congested feelings that are stuck within him or her. However, few know how to do this. Therefore they are automatically spun and woven together into the tapestry you believe is reality, tiny threads of emotions and beliefs that collectively manifest a distorted reality here in the third dimension." Mary paused, then said, "The deeper and muddier the thread, the denser the presence of unresolved emotions and incorrect beliefs, welded together; they stick together in a bond that keeps our focus only on pain and separation in this dimension."

As she continued to talk, Mary began to emanate light all around her. Her eyes brightened, and a luminous silver thread moved between her heart and mine. Something amazing and special was happening, and I didn't want it to end. By now, it was crystal clear to me that Mary really was more than I had imagined.

She continued with her explanation, telling me that she really was not from Earth. She was a cosmic visitor who had come to repair the fabric of life as we believed it to be here in the third dimension. She was weaving light into the darkness of our reality. There were others like her, she said, each one stationed at a different place on Earth, and each one broadcasting light alone from wherever she or he was.

"As we weave light into the fabric of your reality," Mary said, "a gridwork of light is created, like a web that stretches across your planet. Each light draws other lights to it, and as the lights gather and brighten, the people of your planet have an opportunity to see beyond the illusion that has been created by their beliefs."

I was stunned, but I instantly grasped what she meant. Tentatively, I enquired, "Can I weave light, too? Are there others like me who feel alone, wondering why we are here and what is our purpose?"

Gently Mary smiled and reached for my hand. "Of course you can," she replied, her eyes glistening. "The reason you feel alone is because you *are* different; you remember more than most, and it has left you feeling alone. You know things can be different, better than they are, but you feel powerless to change things. Now you can focus on what we have shared together and work to make your own light brighter through your continued conscious choices. This will strengthen your power to make a real difference in your world."

Gingerly I reached to touch the cloth. I wanted to know how much of the radiant beauty I was watching her put into the cloth came from the stars.

Mary read the question in my eyes and said, "Every one of you who works to bring your own light to the surface is a part of this cloth. Your light is woven in here, just as mine is. We are the same. We are beings of light, connected to the stars, even if we are from different places."

She paused and then continued, "As an interstellar traveler, I know how to unravel and reweave the structures of reality into a better form. I'm here to show others how to do that, too. It begins by managing your thoughts and your emotions, seeing the dark that is there, but consciously choosing to bring light into that darkness. The light dissolves the knots of darkness, and the fabric of reality becomes more beautiful as you recognize cosmic truths and the power of your own participation in life through conscious choices."

"You are a woman, and I am a man, Mary. Does that make a difference?" I asked.

She laughed softly, and said, "We are androgynous beings of light. I am in a female form, and you are in a male form, but when we are balanced, we carry a bit of both within us in unity. The divine feminine lives within each of us, just as the divine masculine does. The divine feminine is the master weaver moving each thread into a position where it can receive more light, but the divine masculine points to the knots of darkness, revealing where the work needs to be done. It takes both energies to achieve this. Through the presence of more light, the density of your illusionary reality fades, loosening the constrictions that bind each human soul into the delusions of collective belief. So yes, you can participate in this light weaving just as much as I do."

Mary stopped her fingers from their task, lacing her hands over her heart, allowing her breathing and heartbeat to merge into a single rhythm. Then she explained, "Only when the rhythms of breath and heartbeat are identically matched with Nature's rhythm here on Earth is the power present to perform this fine work of unraveling and reweaving. It means that your thoughts and your feelings must be in alignment, as well as your heartbeat and your breath. When you are unified in intent, you have more power. Positive thoughts alone won't change anything. You must learn to change your thoughts by changing how you *feel*. When you focus upon feeling really happy, you feel much better than when you focus upon what you perceive is wrong in your life. That's why wise people on your planet remind you of the power of laughter. It is impossible to be unhappy or think negative thoughts when you are truly engaged in the real joy of laughter. You must also remember that you are part of Nature, and stop trying to control Nature. The alignment of heart and breath, thoughts and feelings, with the rhythm of your natural world create the precision required for returning a collective thread of light to change your reality to one supported by love."

What Mary was revealing was allowing me to view the fabric of life differently. It was no longer a piece of cloth with radiant lights and dark knots. It was something more. Now I could see that the human knots and storylines were attached through dense, dull threads, binding each person through his or her sticky emotions and beliefs. It was the knots that kept the collective stuck in fear and separation, each person defending the threads that pulled most poignantly against the natural rhythms of her or his own heart.

"Humanity also has an unrealistic and incorrect fascination with time," Mary continued. "And dissolving that fascination is key to making positive change, for most people don't really live in the present moment."

I shook my head, trying to grasp all that she was saying. "Do you mean that we should not consider the past or the future?"

"Consider them to be what they are," Mary suggested. "They are illusions. The future has not arrived yet, so you can only imagine it. The past is already gone, so it no longer exists. If you are working with the power of your thoughts and the power of your feelings, you need to focus on the present moment, for that is all that is real. Everything else is illusion."

That was a bit challenging for me to work out, because I knew that I had to be at work at a specific time, so how could I focus only on the present?

Mary said, "Keep your thoughts in the present, even knowing that there is somewhere you will be in the next present moment. Don't think about work until you are there. Don't think about work after you have come home. But when you are at work, keep all your attention on work because that is your now. That is keeping your thoughts in the present moment."

I saw, now, that time had become the great separator for all of us because we focused upon the history of a past that no longer existed or a fictional future, rather than on what was present right now. Mary and other light weavers were present to unravel the wrong colored threads, shifting them into positions where more light made them both stronger and more resilient in the present moment.

When the threads were rewoven with care and love, the space was created, like a window, where each person could see how she or he had been viewing the world through a veil of illusion. And it was each person's choice to return to the murky, tired, old patterns of their lives or to step into the brilliance of a better and more fulfilling life.

I asked Mary to explain a bit more about how the dark knots were formed so that I could better know how to prevent them, as well as untangle them.

"Your people have focused upon how they are different, rather than how they are alike. They have dulled their senses, turning their thoughts towards an imagined progress they believe they can control. Drinking, smoking, inappropriate sex, and gluttony of all kinds have dulled their sensibilities, and in their stupor, the denseness of their threads is darkened, weaving crooked patterns that oppress and further separate them. They keep themselves busy with the noise of too much conversation, loud music, television, or radio, rather than appreciating the gifts of silence. They have separated themselves from Nature. They have forgotten their power to choose a different way of being in the world, and because they focus upon past and future rather than now, they are shriveled in fear, frightened of what might happen next or remembering the pain of the threads that defined their world before.

"Look at the people around you every day," Mary said. "When you look beneath the surface, you can see that their fear is everywhere; they are driven by a terror that comes from their obsession with time, for if time runs out, they believe they will die and exist no more. They hold on to traumas of the past, and they envision futures that are not always positive."

I now clearly knew what I needed to do. I was one of those pledged to do the work of weaving light back into the pattern, moving everyone towards unity and peace. I thanked Mary, and left with a smile on my face and a new kind of peace in my heart. I knew how each of my present moments from now on would be spent. No matter the challenges, no matter how hard, I would continue making choices of light for the highest good of all, moment by moment.

The next day when I stopped by Mary's after work, she was gone, as were the loom and all of her personal belongings. She had left a note for me on her sewing table.

"Remember," the note said, "You are a weaver of light because you are a being of love."

Pleiadian Christ

"How many years have humans looked for someone else to save them? I am speaking with you now to help you save yourselves." The voice on the hill had drawn thousands of people, and all were curious about who he was and how he had suddenly appeared.

"My name is Jesu," the man said, "and I came from the stars, just like you did. During the time I lived on Earth, people were looking for a messiah to save them from slavery and create a peaceful kingdom. They did not understand that peace can never be created from the outside or provided by someone else. In fact, I've noticed that humans still don't understand this concept; they still look for someone else to create the peace they desire. But peace begins in the heart, and each person is responsible for creating peace within him or herself, which then reflects into the outer environment.

But most people, both then and now, live in internal conflict, full of dissatisfaction and desire, which then radiates out through their thoughts, beliefs, and unsettled emotions to create more conflict, separation, and even war in the outer world.

"When I began to show people what was possible more than two thousand of your years ago, they believed I was the messiah for whom they had been waiting. They watched me achieve what they believed was impossible. They felt the love and peace that radiated from within me into the environment around me. Time and time again, I demonstrated that it was possible for each person to achieve the peace she or he sought, but timid, afraid, and steeped in dysfunctional belief systems, they clung to the idea that they were powerless to do what I was able to do. They believed that I was someone special, someone to be worshipped, the messiah on whom they had been waiting, rather than seeing and understanding that each of them was equally able to perform what they perceived as miracles. They refused to believe that they could achieve peace simply by following the principles I demonstrated and shared through the stories I told them. It is no different today. People still look for religious leaders or psychologists to make them feel peaceful inside or governments or kings to save them from the conflicts that exist in the external world. They look for other people to change so that they can feel love, rather than recognizing that love is already within them. It is very clear to me that many people on this planet are still looking to governments, religions, or other leaders (often the very ones who *create* the problems, conflicts, and separation) to *resolve* these same problems and conflicts. Their partners and families do not change to make them happy; their leaders, whether kings or popes are not saving the people from suffering, and they never will.

"There are two reasons that I can see this so clearly. First, I have no inner conflict within me, so my intuition and my vision are clear and aligned with cosmic truth. There is no veil of illusion over what I can see. Second, my perspective is much broader because I do not share the beliefs of limitation that humans hold because they continually think of themselves as separate from the divine, the source of all possibilities. I know that they are divine themselves, yet they have forgotten that.

"Actually, I came from the Pleiadian star system."

There were gasps in the crowd as they took this in.

"I was one of the last Pleiadians to walk among humans in a form similar to your own. We no longer do that because after several attempts over many centuries to show you how to activate your own powers of creation and achieve a peaceful kingdom, we learned that you were simply unable to see yourselves as the great beings that you are. For some reason, you continue to believe that we are gods or that we have magical powers you do not possess. It is not our wish to be seen as separate or different from you; we have only wanted to support your evolution and to show you that you can achieve what we can achieve—in every way! I came to teach by example, to demonstrate two very basic principles that would bring the kingdom of peace humans seem unable to achieve. I will share those two principles in a moment, since even now, you have failed to master them. But first, I want to explain more fully that my coming was nothing unusual.

"For thousands of years interstellar beings of a higher wisdom and vibration have visited Earth in attempts to show your struggling species how to move beyond your karma. Karma is created by making unconscious choices without consideration of the two cosmic laws that bring peace. Karma is not something that you have to live through to be punished or to gain experience. Once you recognize, know, and honor the two basic cosmic laws, karma ceases to exist because each choice you make is made for the highest good of all.

"When I came to your planet, the people of Earth were trapped in an illusion of their own making, unable to see how to change their thoughts, their beliefs, and their behaviors so that they could begin to live like cosmic citizens. They misunderstood the principle of Duality, believing it to be a point of separation rather than a lens through which to see other perspectives for a greater picture of the whole. People saw anything that was different as a threat, and so they created enemies all around them. They did not possess the ability to be curious about differences and learn from them. And so, they continually created an illusion of separation as they fought, judged, and suffered. I came to eliminate that suffering, if I could, by showing them another way. I wanted them to remember the essence of love that lives in each heart and show them that each person carries a divine spark of light that is interconnected, both here on Earth and in the Universe. Alas, they refused to release their judgments, their beliefs, and their tribal loyalty. Unfortunately, people on your planet still cling rigidly to the beliefs that separate you, rather than embracing the principles that could advance your development.

"The greatest loyalty is never loyalty to family, religion, government, or whatever god you may worship. These things are based on belief systems that create more and more separation because they focus upon what is *different* as a threat. These so-called loyalties create conflict because they are created from an illusion of reality rather than from the clear perspective of an intuitive heart's wisdom. The greatest loyalty surpasses all of these so-called loyalties, for it is connected to Source, cosmic perspectives, and divine wisdom. The greatest loyalty you can achieve is loyalty to the Truth—not your imagined truth based upon so-called facts or teachings that have been handed down from generation to generation, but on *real* universal Truth based upon cosmic laws.

"The two principles humans need to learn, understand, and embody to achieve your highest evolutionary state, becoming cosmic citizens, are very simple. Through the centuries these principles have been given many names by the mystics who could see through your illusionary system, but the essence of these two vital concepts is the same. I will use the terms here that are most pleasing to hear and most familiar to you in this time, so that you can better grasp them. The first is easily expressed by the Sanskrit word *Ahimsa.*" Now he sang the sounds and explained, "*Ah* is a heart sound. *Him* is a sound of safety and nurturance. *Sa* is a sound sending peace out to others. Say it out loud, " he continued. *"Ahimsa.* Doesn't the sound automatically generate a sense of inner peace? The tones contained in this beautiful word incorporates the most important aspect of life. It simply means, *"Do No Harm."* People today seem to grasp this concept at a mental level, but most people fail to act on that knowing because the truth of *Ahimsa* does not live in their hearts. They are simply not guided by rules for living that promote the highest good for all—the most necessary principle for a peaceful kingdom. Full of separating ideas such as competition and judgment, people attack others who are not like them or believe that there is not enough of everything for everyone;

and so, they compete against one another, which leads to trickery and lies, taking what is not theirs, and filling them full of fear that they will lose what they have. This way of living is far from concepts that create a peaceful kingdom. *Do no harm* means do not harm *anything* or *anyone.* As a simple example, honoring a belief system that dictates that people can kill animals for food causes great harm both to the animals that are killed and to the people that eat the animals. It is obvious to me that the animals experience much fear and pain when they are killed. But what humans fail to see is that they are ingesting the energy of this same fear and pain when they eat the killed animal. Believing that this is necessary for nurturing the human form is absurd, for you are not taking in nutrients; you are taking in the energy of death, which will lead to your own demise."

Some of the crowd now started to squirm uncomfortably, but Jesu continued. "Perhaps some of you may have heard stories of my teaching about the lion lying down with the lamb? This example was intended to show you that violence does not resonate with higher consciousness. How conscious is it to choose the energy of pain, fear, and death as a form of nurturance for your body? Plants, on the other hand, offer their nurturance without killing the plant. Nature offers all that you need to sustain yourselves, but you still choose to kill for your food. And when you believe that killing for food is acceptable, it is easy for you to extend that belief to feeling that killing another person (or persons) whose ideas threaten you in some way, is also acceptable. Thus, you have war. Human dysfunctional belief systems have caused you to become arrogant, believing that you are more important than other expressions of life. You are not. Each life is precious, and no human has the right to harm anyone or anything else, whether it is an animal or another person.

"*Ahimsa* also means do no harm through your thoughts or your emotions. You are responsible for what you think, which radiates to all others. You are also responsible for how you manage your emotions. In the Pleiades, we call your human emotions "signposts," for they point to how *you* are out of balance, giving you an opportunity to change your thinking about whatever is occurring, and guiding you back into a state of grace and flow, if you follow their directions and return to your center, rather than judging and blaming others for what you are feeling. You are responsible for correcting how you feel when your emotions show you that it is *you* who is out of balance with your heart, not someone else who is doing something you perceive to be wrong. How conscious are you if you constantly worry or dwell on negative thoughts, always blaming someone else or something else for your own suffering? How conscious are you if you refuse to heed your own emotional messages?

"*Ahimsa* also means do no harm to your precious body. Choices of smoking, drinking alcohol, eating sugar (an addictive drug more harmful than cocaine or heroin), or taking other drugs are harming the body where your essence resides on this planet. Do no harm means to be conscious of every behavior and every choice you make personally. Do no harm means causing no harm to anything or anyone, including yourself. When you can live your lives through honoring the principles of *Ahimsa*, you will make an evolutionary leap in raising your consciousness and your vibration, and you will move towards peace."

Jesu could see more people were arriving, curious and interested in what he had to say. He amplified his voice to reach them all. "The second core principle I came to instill into human consciousness is the idea that everything and everyone are connected. You are energy. Everything around you is energy. Therefore, everything you think or do affects everything and everyone else. When the Pleiadians visited and lived with the Mayans for a while, the Maya called this principle *In Lak'ech*, which means, "I am another yourself." If you recognize the truth in this, you can stop separating yourself from others, competing with them, judging them, or making war on them. The principle of *In Lak'ech* means that you are no different from anyone else. Each person has different gifts, abilities, and perspectives that can be shared with the whole of humanity. You may have a different personal story, but the essence of each of you is the same. You are divine sparks of light, intended to share your light with others. When I was living on Earth, I shared this concept by using myself as an example and saying, "What you do to the least of these brothers or sisters, you do to me."

"That saying explains the essential meaning of *In Lak'ech*. If you harm someone else, you harm yourself. If you cause harm to yourself, you are harming others. I so hoped humanity could grasp these simple concepts, which interweave and support each other. They are the basics required for cosmic citizenship and for recognizing the rules of the Universe. Alas, even two thousand years later, you are still killing animals for food, judging one another, competing rather than cooperating with each other, speaking harmful, emotional words in outbursts of hatred, jealousy, anger, and fear, and killing each other in senseless wars. You are, indeed, stuck, as a species.

"As I mentioned, Pleiadians and other inter-stellar friends of the human species have visited Earth often, attempting to remove the veil of forgetfulness and show the people all of what they are capable of accomplishing. But each time, rather than summoning their own courage to step out-side of their beliefs or to change their patterns of emotional reaction and behavior, the people of each epoch made the mistake of believing that we were gods, rather than friends who were simply showing them another way. In short, they refused to believe in their own power, in their own ability to make good choices moment by moment, or in their own divine creative gifts. From the Maya to the Cherokee to the Australian Aborigines to the Siberian shamans, some people received and integrated the wisdom of possibilities, becoming sages who continued the interstellar work of teaching by example on Earth. But most humans are full of fear, stubborn, and lazy. They are afraid of being judged if they change the way they have always done things. They are afraid of not being loved. And so, they resolutely cling to their tribal mentality of separation, judgment, and suffering, when the possibility for a different reality is right in front of them. This was true over five thousand years ago when the Pleiadians worked with the Maya, two thousand years ago when I was on Earth, and it is true today. People simply refuse to take responsibility for their own choices, and they continue to obstinately hold on to the idea that someone *else* is going to save them."

Now some people had puzzled looks on their faces, and others looked completely abashed. Realizing that he was reaching some of them, he began again. "When I came to Earth, the Pleiadian Elders Council had decided it was time to try again. They asked who would like to make a trip to once again attempt to show humanity the true reality and the pathway to cosmic citizenship? I was excited about the possibility! I volunteered, and several other essences agreed to come with me to play human roles to which, we hoped, the people of Earth could relate. But once again people refused to see the truth. The loving essence who agreed to be my mother was not recognized for her own wisdom. Once the people decided that I was their messiah and the one who would save them, they stepped into the same tired, old pattern of considering me a god. The essence playing the role of my mother was dismissed for her own worth and value, for according to the rules of the times, women were not valuable for their own gifts or wisdom; she was appreciated merely as the vessel who gave life to their god. Her many examples of wisdom were simply cast aside, as all attention was turned on me. I was the one doing magical practices; I performed things they just could not seem to do themselves simply because they refused to practice what I showed them. They could not imagine that they, too, held the power to make such magical changes." Jesu noticed some people in the crowd were nervously fingering crosses they wore around their necks. Hoping he was reaching them, he provided some examples.

"When I turned water into wine at a wedding, the people stood in awe, grateful for the wine. They missed the lesson that one thing always affects another. Of course, the residue of wine in the casks flavored the water, giving it also the taste of wine. And the more they drank, the less they could discern between wine-flavored water and wine. I showed them the power of belief when I did that, but they did not realize the truth.

"When I was credited with healing the sick, I was showing people the power of compassion and love. Those who were healed actually healed themselves because they believed it was possible, not because of anything I mystically achieved. Anyone can heal himself or herself, if he or she trusts in their own power and removes the effects of trauma held in the body and emotions. It is the scars of trauma, little or big, that continue to cause imbalance or sickness. I wanted people to know that they could be healed and whole through changing themselves, without the aid of another person or a god. I also wanted them to know that extending compassion and unconditional love is the most supportive medicine anyone can offer, for it raises the vibration of both the one giving and the one receiving.

Now it was time to share the truth about others who had joined him in his mission so long ago. "The essence who suffered the most when we Pleiadians walked the earth two thousand years ago was the one who agreed to accompany me as my earthly wife, known today as Mary Magdalene. Because she was a female, she, too, was dismissed and maligned. Her great power of love and forgiveness was rejected. And because the people had been taught there could be only one god, it was impossible for them to view her as having the same powers and wisdom as I did, even though she demonstrated those powers on a regular basis! If I was their one chosen god, then she could only be mortal. They dismissed the wisdom of everything she demonstrated, most especially, how to love unconditionally. She suffered because of that, and I am truly sorry, although I tried my best to dissuade the people from their rigid and inappropriate beliefs and behaviors. No matter how much we tried together to demonstrate that their beliefs were incorrect, they refused to accept the truth.

"At last, my time on Earth came to an end, and my wife and mother returned to the Pleiades some years after I did. My leaving was turned into a story that proved to the people that I had, indeed, been a god, thereby negating *all* of our work to show that each person could do the same things I did. The process of ascension through choosing higher vibratory energy became a story of a religious ritual that could only be attained by a god. That belief remains today, although with continual proper higher vibratory choices, anyone can ascend as I did. Today many religions imply that a person cannot even talk directly to their god without a priest's intervention, much less emulate the feats that I demonstrated."

People were exchanging glances, trying to figure out what to think.

"After we returned to our home, the Pleiadians watched and waited to see if our visit had made an impact on the evolution of humanity. Sadly, the people separated even more after our departure, warring against each other in my name now and causing even more destruction to your planet. We hoped that time would bring wisdom to your floundering species, but even the passage of time on Earth did little to bring you to a place of recognizing the true reality.

"After thousands of years of interstellar guidance, the Pleiadians and other star councils decided to take another approach. There would be no more walking among the humans as friends or demonstrating what is possible; we would simply telepathically share potentials for change with those whose vibration had evolved enough to resonate with the truth and to receive our guidance. We had to trust that some of you were developing quickly enough to grasp these seeds of wisdom and begin to use the power of a developing consciousness. But once again, we miscalculated what was possible within the human personality. While many received the wisdom and truth, they immediately claimed it as their own, deciding that they were now the special teachers, leaders, or healers. They competed with one another for status and position rather than helping others through sharing this wisdom. They were stuck again, and we watched in desperation, for every day that they continued on the path of competition and separation, was a day they did further damage to the planet and the energy around Earth.

"They were still missing the essential knowledge that thoughts—all thoughts—are energy, and energy can either harm or help everyone, for everything is connected. Nor did they take advantage of the emotions that were their signposts for change within themselves. Further, they refused to move beyond the mental realm that they so highly prized; they simply would not allow their thoughts to be led by the wisdom of the heart. They were mired in a swamp of emotion and personality that eclipsed the essence of who they were. Cooperation worked only as long as the ones cooperating felt they were in control. The moment conflict arose, they moved back into judgment, blame, and separation, and the thoughts that flew out of them when being challenged were dangerously altering the environment. How could the ones who considered themselves to be special leaders help the collective of humanity, which was even more trapped by illusion, if those who called themselves teachers, leaders, and healers insisted that they were special (a form of separation) by claiming only they were right or that they were better than those they taught? They failed to realize that being *different* did not mean being *special*. It meant different. We were dismayed to watch the energy of human thought continuing to pollute the region around the planet. Because energy travels not only across your planet, but also through the cosmos, we saw that this negative environment would soon expand to contaminate the entire universe. We could not let that happen.

"And so, the decision was made. We began to beam the energy of pure love and light directly into the heart of the discord. The people were even more frightened by the presence of so much light. Their physical bodies, which housed all their previous discord and trauma, began to get sick, as the trauma rose to the surface for healing. We continued to beam in the higher vibrations, even though the people suffered. They needed to either adapt to the higher vibrational energy of light, or their physical bodies would die. Our purpose was to prevent them from destroying the planet, while opening their hearts to expand their conscious awareness and help them to better understand the true nature of reality. As some of them adapted, they stopped the old patterns of negative thinking and reactive behaviors. That was wonderful to watch! And so, we continued to beam in the higher vibrational light.

"Gradually, a small number of humans began to respond. Although they, like the others, were physically sick, at a deeper level they realized that they were simply changing. We worked with their High Self Angels to pour dreams and visions into their consciousness to help them understand how to let go of what they believed to be real and embrace a larger truth. Ever so slowly, these few began to heal themselves. As they released old traumas from their bodies, the light was no longer so harsh to them. They changed their patterns of thought, feelings, and behaviors. They began to see themselves and all others with compassion, finally recognizing that everyone and everything *is* truly connected. Some of them slowly stopped eating, for their bodies no longer needed food. They discovered that they were being nourished by light and the higher frequencies that were permeating the planet. They were no longer afraid of what was happening, but calmly accepted it, recognizing that they were about to experience magical changes. There were a few who were able to merge with our energy and transmit messages to others from the wisdom we shared. Those who worked in pairs filtered out any personal beliefs about our messages, so their transmissions were real and true.

The expressions throughout the crowd were shifting. Some showed relief; some were becoming disinterested. Some showed a deeper comprehension.

Jesu pressed on. "But not enough people were interested in listening to our messages or changing their beliefs about themselves, their perceived reality, or what was happening in their world. Most of the population continued their old habits and beliefs. Therefore, the world continued to spiral downward into the lower and lower energies.

"Most people continued to live in fear and self-ishness, in spite of the high energies we contin-ued to send to the planet. As they clung to their old behaviors and their consciousness continued to drop, they turned their attention more and more towards the illusions they believed to be real, which made them very easy to control by other powers that wished to destroy humanity.

"Listen, 'he said. "Eventually, the dynamic tension between the people with low vibratory consciousness and the few who have very high vibratory consciousness will cause a pop that rip-ples throughout the universe. We call this the

Cosmic Pop that will save humanity, and we are warning you who are listening that the Cosmic Pop is approaching. I am speaking to you now in a final appeal to take responsibility to save yourselves.

"When it finally happens, those who have been plunging into lower, denser levels of awareness will be removed to another place where you can continue your karmic lessons without harming the Earth. Those who are becoming more light-filled will experience a heightened awareness where you will recognize your cosmic brothers and sisters, your true spiritual family. You will work together in harmony, each offering your individual gifts for the whole as every decision is made through the core principles of Ahimsa and In Lak'ech. You will find you are living in an ascending New Earth, which has split apart from the denser third-dimensional reality with which you were familiar. Now you will be able to experience the lightness and beauty and freedom of everything we Pleiadians have tried to teach humanity for so long. The dense physical forms to which you were accustomed will began to fade, and you will experience being lighter and freer. As you dramatically transform into waves of energy, you will begin to think where you wish to be, and instantly you will be there. You will be joyful, for you will no longer fear what others think or what might happen to you. There will be no past, no future, only the now moment. With your deepening sense of connection to all life, you as new humans will move together with the New Earth in a unified wave as the planet ascended to a new position in the council of stars. You will be free to explore new assignments and new adventures, supported by your interstellar friends.

"It is a shame that so many humans are choosing to continue their karmic lessons and patterns somewhere else, but it has always been their choice. The wave of destructivity must be contained so that the Universe is no longer being contaminated. And it is most fortunate that some of the more enlightened of you are willing to listen, to make necessary changes, and to step into cosmic citizenship as the New Humans! Our work is now complete, and we will be pleased to greet our brothers and sisters, who will soon join us in helping other species who are as stuck as humanity has been. We have finally, after thousands of years, succeeded in helping those of you who wish to change and evolve, and we will simultaneously save the Earth. Thank you for listening."

Jesu suddenly disappeared, and the crowd began to slowly disperse. There was an obvious split between those who were retreating into their old patterns of thought and behavior, considering this experience just an entertaining moment, and those who were already beginning to change. The first group was dense and darker, while the other group was much more light-filled. As they moved in separate directions, Jesu looked back and smiled. It was done.

Integration

The essence of Joysong thrust itself against the human container that felt completely foreign to her. It felt like someone else. How had she managed to suddenly be inside such a limited vehicle? Trapped! She was stuck inside a little girl named Vinnie who wiggled and squirmed and tried to resolve Joysong's deep discomfort. Realizing that she was now occupying the same physical space as the little girl, Joysong suddenly understood the changes she had undergone. For one thing, she was no longer androgynous; her essence was now female. She stopped pushing against the little girl and stopped resisting the fact that she was caught in this untenable situation, trying to simply align with the child's breathing. She couldn't remember how she got here; her memory had been fading ever since she first arrived. Human words were erasing the truth she remembered in her heart—human words that contained foreign ideas and rules that people all around her continued to repeat to her. It was made very clear to her that if she did not follow the rules, there would be severe consequences.

Joysong felt isolated and alone. Her body would not do what she knew was possible. She wanted to simply wish herself someplace else, someplace more pleasant with kinder people. She missed the gentle tones of a softer and more beautiful language than the language these humans used. Oh, she remembered....she was now human, too, now that she was trapped inside this little girl. The words others insisted Joysong learn to repeat did not approach the beauty of the melodious tones she was accustomed to using for communication. She tried to communicate with Vinnie, but the child was confused and afraid because people were constantly telling her she was wrong or trying to control her. Joysong tried to let her know that she was part of the child and could teach her ways to get around the rules. But instead, as she desperately tried to merge their two awarenesses together, she found that she was actually forgetting who she was rather than helping Vinnie to remember. Flying, the freedom of instantly being wherever she wanted to be, communicating telepathically, and feeling love all around her—these things were simply slipping away. She tried to teach Vinnie how to fly and bruised her knees. She closed her eyes tight and thought about her favorite place, intending to travel there, but when she opened them, she was still sitting in the child's bedroom. She tried to send Vinnie's mother a message that she wanted a hug, but the mother was too busy or merely unable to tune into telepathic messages. Joysong knew she had been safe and loved before she merged her essence with this little girl, but now she felt unseen, unrecognized, unloved, and controlled. It was horrible. She just could not be or do what she still slightly remembered. And she didn't like the way people referred to her by this stupid name, "Vinnie." It was distasteful. Her name was Joysong.

When she was a bit older, the big people called parents took Vinnie to a concrete building called a school every day and made her sit on a hard chair and listen to other big people talk about things neither the teachers nor the students understood. Joysong knew better. They were wrong, but they insisted they were right, and they gave Vinnie grades according to how much she agreed with them and could repeat it. Vinnie was good at memorizing what they needed to hear and repeating it, but it did not resonate with what Joysong knew was true.

Gradually, Joysong realized that, for now, she and Vinnie were one. She sat all day, stealing glimpses out of the window into the freedom that awaited her. The trees outside the school window seemed to laugh, knowing that she would escape to climb into their branches the moment she was released from her daily prison. When the bell rang announcing that she was free to go, she ran as fast as her little legs would carry her, past the mothers and fathers who came to carry their children home. Luckily, she lived near enough to the school to walk home, and her mother allowed that, as long as she didn't take too long. She always managed to measure her time well enough to allow climbing into the branches of her favorite tree, midway between the school and her house. There she could breathe. She listened to the birds and squirrels around her and she sent messages of love back to them without words. When she was in the tree, she could properly communicate.

Days, then years passed as Joysong-Vinnie struggled to find ways to control her own life. Although she knew that she was so much more than simply a little girl here on this planet, to the others she was still just a growing child. Her mother constantly fidgeted with her clothes, adjusting and correcting the shoes that would not stay tied or the blouse that came loose as she ran and played. All the while, her mother was explaining how she had to look pretty and behave well to be loved. Every night her father summarized her errors of the day and sternly told her she had to do better. It was impossible. Joysong was doing the best she could in this foreign place and inside this limiting body of Vinnie. As she went to sleep each night, she asked and asked and asked to be taken home. It seemed nobody was listening. Perhaps the communication pathways had been partially broken when she arrived on this planet. But sometimes friends from the other realms would come and take her away for a short while to a place where she felt safe and loved; she was restored while she was there. But they always brought her back before morning, and the next day only brought more of the same patterns and a general lack of control over her own life.

For years, Joysong-Vinnie tried to fit into the world simply as Vinnie. She even stopped thinking about her essence as Joysong, trying to become just "Vinnie." She did her best to follow the rules, but no matter what she did, it was never enough, or she got it wrong according to everyone else. She found herself trusting the wrong people when she opened her heart, forgetting that everyone was not as light-filled as she was. So she got hurt. But that was nothing new. Her parents, her teachers, even those who called themselves her friends were always criticizing her and telling her to stop dreaming. Being told she was wrong or not good enough was just part of her everyday experience here in this place. She really wanted to go home where she could fully be who she was and where she was appreciated and loved just for being herself.

She spent as much time in Nature as she could, for that was the only place she found solace or could feel free. In the woods, fairies and little people talked to her. Forest creatures never judged her. Nor were any of them frightened by her song or the way she gently moved around them. She had friends of all kinds in the woods—a fox and her kits, several deer, badgers and porcupines, birds, squirrels, and of course, the fairies and little people no one else seemed to be able to see. Twice she had even had the pleasure of talking with a bear. It was digging for food as it traveled through the forest when she found it one sunny afternoon. Neither the bear nor the child was startled by each other's presence. They simply sniffed each other and accepted each other. The next day the bear was still there, so she was able to thank it for coming to see her.

Vinnie knew that everyone was related—plants, animals, people, for they were all energy expressing in a particular form. Therefore, there was nothing to fear, and communication was easy. She simply sent messages of love and acceptance from her heart. Sometimes she spent long hours sitting on a rock by the stream that ran through the woods. As she listened to the song of the water moving downstream, she could barely remember that she, too, used to move like this, flowing around obstacles and bringing her song everywhere she went. She waited, day by day for years, hoping each day would bring the magic required to return her home. Every night when she went to sleep, she asked to be set free.

After she was grown, Vinnie was visiting another town, and something magical happened. She saw another essence like herself! It was the first time in her life that she had seen another person who openly carried an essence like she did. Only this one was in a male form. Eagerly she approached him with a smile. She introduced herself using her earthly name. He introduced himself as Devin. His smile was unlike any she had encountered, and instantly she could feel his very big heart. She realized that he, too, was a free essence like herself trapped in a human body. The two essences were drawn together mysteriously, and Devin and she began a relationship the moment they met. There was no human story required; they simply recognized each other and knew who they were separately and together. She told him her real name, and he smiled. He could see her, and that was enough for her.

Devin told her his real name and about his standing and looking out the window as a child and asking to be taken home. She immediately understood that he had come here knowing the same things she did. She shared how her friends used to take her away to a safe and happy place during the night as a child, only to bring her back before morning. Because people in his life had not tried so hard to change or control him, Devin remembered more of what was possible. He remembered everything—well, almost everything. He knew it was possible to walk through walls and to be everywhere at once, but like her, he was blocked from doing that now. He knew how to communicate telepathically, but that also did not seem to work so well with other people. He had as many animal friends as she did. She remembered and shared with him the unconditional love that naturally exists everywhere in the universe— except, of course, on this planet where they were now. They decided that they would have to re-create that unconditional love together on this planet.

Vinnie and Devin spent hours trying to unravel the mystery of why they were here and were unable to accomplish all the things they knew were possible. Truthfully, they were both puzzled about why they were here if they were unable to be who they were or do what they knew was possible. Living on this planet was painful with the knowledge of how much better things *could* be.

They both spent time every day talking to their friends from other realms and other dimensions, whether they were Angelic, Devic, animal, or interstellar. These contacts had more meaning than their human relationships, except, of course, with each other. Sometimes they got answers to their many questions, but not always. They tried to live their lives through unconditional love to demonstrate to others who were struggling or wanted a better world where all the things they knew were possible.

Years went by as Vinnie and Devin moved from place to place, trying to make the world better. People they encountered did not seem to be interested in the kinds of changes they longed for. So they did what they could for those who wanted little changes, and they connected more deeply with those who were more open to the big changes that were possible with awakening to higher awareness.

Awakening. That was what was needed. People needed to wake up and see the true reality. They needed to make choices from their hearts rather from the bad training they had received to fit into the world as it was.

One day they were in their favorite place with the huge trees and bears all around. They were sitting in a meadow playing with a bear cub when the mother bear came and telepathically invited them to come to another part of the woods. They eagerly got up and followed the bear to see what wonder was awaiting them. They walked for a couple of hours, going deeper and deeper into the forest. Finally the bear led them to a huge flat rock that overlooked a ravine. There was a lake at the bottom, and the water looked cool and inviting. The bear gave them a gentle push towards the edge. They looked harder and began to make out the slight outline of a craft hovering over the water. They could see bright wavelike forms floating outside the craft. The bear gave another gentle nudge and looked at them intently. Stopping to listen to their bear friend's telepathic message, they slowly began to realize that something wonderful was happening. The bear was pointing out to them that there were others like them over the lake. Then the bear stood up on its hind legs and roared to get the attention of the other beings nearby, who turned and quietly floated toward Devin and Vinnie standing at the edge of the cliff. A peaceful feeling preceded the arrival of these beings, and Vinnie and Devin both had an instant recall of who was approaching. The bear began to back up and move toward the forest path, but not before thanking Vinnie and Devin for the time they had spent together over the years and the kindness they had showed her cubs. Vinnie and Devin said good-bye to their bear friend and turned their full attention on the beings who were now almost at the edge of the rock where they were standing.

Beckoning to Vinnie and Devin to join them, the others waved and showed them where they should walk. Stunned, Vinnie and Devin hesitated for only a moment before realizing that the edge of the cliff was now somehow magically connected to a rainbow colored pathway extending from where they stood all the way to the craft over the lake. Without question, they joined hands, stepped off the cliff, and began walking towards the water. The others moved to let them pass, smiling and touching them as they moved toward the lake. At the end of the path, they found they were hovering over the water. Laughing, they introduced themselves to the others—this time not by their earthly names, but by tones they emitted from their hearts.

After introductions, they were invited into the craft and offered the opportunity to come home with them.

The bear had turned back to the cliff's edge after Vinnie and Devin had walked away. Watching now with a wise look in her eyes, she sent them a fond farewell as she watched the ship slowly ascend from the lake and move into the sky.

Orion

I had never felt I belonged on this Earth, and having frequently claimed as much to my tolerant and amused friends, it surprised no one when I took advantage (to my way of thinking) of a class on the existence of extra-terrestrial beings. The teacher, Agmorha Benaway, was holding the class on Tuesday nights at the local college. Most of the students were sophomores and juniors trying to earn some easy credit, but they didn't seem to mind a middle-aged lady in their ranks. After all, I prided myself on being "with it," and they easily accepted me.

We spent the first few weeks examining all the current scientific data for the possibility of life on other planets. We saw slides taken from the US Viking of Mars and from the Soviet Venera of Venus, and I filled my notebook with the chemical components of poisonous vapors and temperature ranges too hot or too cold to bear life. My margins, however, were filled with my penciled depictions of the possibilities that awaited us. My artistic flair knew no limits on this subject.

Sometime around the fourth week of class, one of my younger classmates managed to divert the teacher, and we embarked on a lively discussion of so-called "sightings." After a two-hour debate, it was decided that the class would visit a documented site of some notoriety, just over the state line in Mississippi. There were multiple reports from various sources about unusual occurrences there, and I was excited to see what we would discover. The time for our field trip was fixed, and before I knew it, we were on our way.

We arrived and settled into our shared rooms at a motel near the site, girls (and me) sharing with girls, and boys sharing with boys. Although we wanted to go straight out to see the site, the teacher insisted we rest until dinner, and then we would venture to the site together. And it was, after all, not even dark yet. So we dutifully rested for a couple of hours. My roommate spent her rest time entirely on her phone. I read. At seven, everyone met for dinner, where the talk was entirely around what many of the students were certain we were going to see—a craft from another planet. I ate my grilled cheese sandwich and fries in eager anticipation of what we might discover that night. And then it was time to go.

Excitement ran high, as the starry-eyed girls dashed into the meadow hoping tonight they would see a "UFO." The boys nervously laughed and teased them. I have a tendency to be a loner, and as usual, I managed to separate myself from the group and wander away. My musings on the possibilities of extra-terrestrial life seemed to guide my feet until I found myself within sound, but not sight, of the others. I sat down to smell, feel, and enjoy the night air, breathing deeply and thinking of all the lonely times I had experienced in my life.

Gazing through the brush toward the meadow beyond, I saw a slight wind stir the trees, and I noticed the trees were moving only in one place. As I watched for a moment, I thought I saw an almost imperceptible line separating the trees; it seemed to somehow divide the trees on one side and the trees on the other and allow the wind to move through between them. Slowly I got up, enthralled with what I thought I was seeing. I approached the hazy, unusual area cautiously at first and then began moving faster to see if I could touch the "line." As I moved toward it, my curiosity drew me on faster and faster until, almost running, I tripped on a rock.

Instantly, I found myself in a very strange environment. I shook my head and tried to see clearly; it seemed that I had been thrust through what seemed to be an invisible door to another world. Something shifted, and suddenly I found myself being propelled down, or through, a long apparently endless corridor. The walls felt like velvet as I brushed by them. Whirling around and around, weightlessly, I found I was traveling swiftly toward a light, but I could not tell what was causing the light.

Abruptly the corridor ended. Unable to stop my forward momentum, I expected to be harshly ejected onto a hard surface, but instead I found myself almost gently blown toward the center of a enormous room. I struggled to gather my bearings, but it was useless. Trying to right myself and put my feet on the ground, I found I was already right side up. I felt as if everything had come unglued, and I continued to float around the room.

As I gave up struggling to reach the ground to stand, I began to relax, and breathe deeply. I allowed myself to simply accept my position, whatever or wherever it might be. In the space of one breath, my vision cleared, and looking around, I saw to my surprise hundreds of glowing forms, shifting and turning. I thought I discerned smiles of a sort.

The glowing, amorphous forms I could now see melded into one another, strange shifting shapes, weird yet so familiar, floating effortlessly through space, into and out of contact with each other. I realized they were beginning to encircle me—a circle I could reach through, which shifted as I tried to touch the various parts of it. They laughed, not a cruel or mocking laugh, but warm ripples of sound that washed over and through me—gentle sounds of amusement and welcome.

The closer the forms within the circle pressed around me, the more obscure they became as I tried to ascribe boundaries to the entities within the circle. In unison, they started to speak, and I heard not words of any sort but deep resonating tones of varying range. The joint chorus quieted, as each being spoke individually. As they spoke, I turned toward each speaker and found I understood their tonal language.

With excitement, they turned various shades and hues of color as they changed their inflection and stressed their points. The arena was alive with vibrating colors, brighter and more alive than any rainbow and softer than the most delicate flower. I could not explain the new sense of pleasure I was feeling, and I began to cry uncontrollably. I realized that this place, these beings were familiar, connected, and comforting to me. It may have seemed strange to others, but to me, it felt like something I had longed for all of my life. Tears of happiness flowed down my face as freely as the forms moving around me. I finally recognized them —I was home, home!

My school group would find only a shell of a body the next morning when they looked for me. They would assume I had hit my head and died instantly. But I knew the truth. I wasn't in that body. I was with my family on Orion.

The Fairy

This is a one-sided story, but it's my story. I should know because I'm the fairy...or at least I was. For reasons that will unfold, I will tell this story from the viewpoint of someone watching. Listen carefully now.

Once upon a time there was a happy fairy, or at least *mostly* happy. She had her moments (when an animal or a plant was hurt or when a human's energy field got too close to her own), but generally her heart was borne up by the lightness of her spirit. One of her favorite pastimes was playing in the woods. She felt at home there. She listened to the trees sing in the wind, and she talked to the rabbits. She dipped her feet into shallow pools of sunny brooks and listened to the water, for it always told her something. She danced through the meadows, full of fairy light, and her light brought all manner of forest dwellers towards her. She was happy.

One day, a human came into the forest, and as usual when humans appeared, she hid. Peeping out from behind a Trillium leaf, she watched him. He was curious. Unlike other humans she had encountered, he seemed to know that the forest was alive. He gazed at the meadow as if he were part of it, something she had never seen a human do before. He was careful where he walked, and he did not fill up the air with idle whistling. He was very, very quiet. She watched as he spoke to the rabbits, her rabbits, and told them that he loved them.

The fairy moved closer to try to understand this human. She flew to a Stargazer Lily and crept to the very edge of a delicate petal. She knew she was in a precarious place, but she could not help herself— she was entranced. From where she stood on the edge of the petal, she strained to see his eyes. They were soft and beautiful, but full of intensity. Two pools of unfathomable depth. Something about him felt familiar and intriguing at the same time. Leaning out farther and farther, she suddenly lost her balance and tumbled forward. The fairy was so surprised that she forgot to use her wings and landed on the ground beneath her with a thump. She sat there, thankful that no one had seen her. Humans never saw her. They some-times felt her energy, saw a beam of her light, or felt the wind from her wings, but they never really saw her. Knowing she was invisible, she continued to sit there, pondering what it was about this human that was different.

He turned from looking at the brook and gazed directly at her. "Are you OK?" he asked.

Stunned that he could actually see her, she could only nod her head. Not only had he seen her, but he had *spoken to her!* She was so flabbergasted that she didn't move. She didn't dare. She simply didn't know what to do.

The human gently put his hand out towards her, offering to help her up. She slowly rose, dusting off her wings, and moved towards his open hand. For some reason beyond her understanding, she climbed onto his hand and nestled into the cupped niche he made for her. She was disoriented by his presence. She was so shocked that he could *see* her and had spoken to her that her heart began to flutter.

Most humans don't know that fairies are empathic. The more she became aware of what she was feeling, the more she realized that she was also feeling what *he* was feeling. This human had a very big and open heart. She knew that instantly, from the moment she stepped into his palm. There was so much love flowing from him that she felt lightheaded. "He smells good," she noticed. Then, tired from her ordeal, she fell asleep in his hand.

Several hours later, the fairy slowly awakened. She blinked in confusion, and then, with awe she realized she had actually gone to sleep in the hands of a human! He was so very still and patient holding her; the feeling of safety penetrated her deeply. In her very long life, she had never been able to go to sleep feeling completely safe. The fairy world can be a dangerous place when humans get too near. Usually she slept much like a dolphin does, with part of her resting and part of her watchful for whatever threats might arise. She needed always to be prepared for flight. What magic did *this* human hold that he could sit motionless for hours patiently watching over her, offering her safety for the first time in all her years on Earth?

He waited for her cue, and when she turned her own soft eyes towards him, he asked with kindness, "What do you need? How can I help you?"

She thought for a moment and answered, "I need to understand who you are. Your heart offers so much to the world, you must be very special. May I stay with you for a while?"

She waited to see if he had heard and understood her. While she had been able to hear and understand him, she was not sure if he would also be able to do the same.

To her surprise, he answered immediately with what appeared to be delight! She felt shivers all over as he spoke to her again.

"Yes. I've been searching for someone who enjoys the magic of Nature as you do. I can feel what you feel, and it helps me to know you."

She was once again stunned. He was empathic, too!

He told her he needed to prepare a safe place for her to stay with him, and that although he must leave now, they would be together again soon. And so, they parted, soon to meet again, with the promise of a wonderful new relationship held deeply in both of their hearts.

The word "*soon*" has different parameters in human time and fairy time; for a fairy, *soon* is almost immediately. For a human, *soon* is more vague, arriving when circumstances permit. She waited patiently until he arrived in the forest again some days later. The winds sang through both their hearts, promising an undefined yet magical alliance.

Their connection was otherworldly. Although he could not fly, she showed him what she could of her fairy realm, and he took her to other places in Nature that were special to him. They discovered together an extraordinary feeling that they were sure had never existed in the known world before. They lived together spending time between his little cottage on the edge of the meadow and in her forest—a shining example of how a relationship *should* be: unconditional, honest, and fully present. For the first time in her life, she allowed herself to be completely open, to share all that she had to give. For the first time in his life, he allowed himself to be close to another.

Time passed, and for reasons neither of them could explain, they began to struggle. Her fairy qualities seemed to irritate him, and he began to doubt that she was seeing reality the way he did. He became harsh with her when she made a mistake, and his harsh words hurt her; she found herself frequently in tears, a new experience for her. The sweetness of their relationship became tarnished with unmet expectations, miscommunications, and disappointment. He complained often that nothing was like it used to be, without seeing the beauty of what was present. She just cried.

While going into Nature always soothed them both, more and more he began to express a bitterness and anger that she could not comprehend. She began to feel that everything good was slipping away from her. It was a trap from which neither of them knew how to escape. She felt segmented somehow, no longer whole. She had been so open with him and found such joy in their transparency together. Now she felt like she was under the microscope where he critically examined everything about her. Perhaps he was just trying to understand *fairy-ness*, but his examination, cataloging, and historical references took the magic out of her. It was like taking the air out of her lungs. She could no longer breathe.

She did not blame him, yet she did not know how to live under his blanket of constant dissatisfaction. One day, without warning, he started averting his eyes from her. Suddenly, it was as if she didn't exist. She began to slip away without knowing or understanding what was happening to her. She lost her joy and found herself struggling to smile. She woke every morning with a feeling of loss, for she had lost herself. The fairy he met and used to love no longer existed. She was standing in the ashes of a self that was burned to the ground, waiting to see who would rise from the ashes.

And as she waited, hoping for a change, he backed further and further away from her, leaving her utterly confused and alone, no longer sure who she was. Waves of pain washed over her. She was indeed lost. She tried to speak to him about what she was feeling, but he could barely deal with his own emotions, much less understand any of hers. When occasionally she did find the courage and opportunity to talk to him, their exchanges often ended by facing each other defiantly, each digging their heels deeper into entrenched viewpoints. He was attached to making her see how foolish she was, how many mistakes she made, and how her vision was flawed. She was attached to making him see how he made her suffer through his continual criticism, by discounting her reality, and by refusing to believe in possibilities.

She didn't know how to shake off the heavy feelings that weighed her down. She felt like she had been caught in severe dew that prevented her from flying. She had slept too far out on a flower petal before, unprotected, and awakening too soggy to fly. But eventually the sun always dried her off. Once dry, the spark of joy in her heart lifted her and carried her on the wind. But there were no sunny days in their relationship now, and she felt no joy.

One morning when she could bear it no longer, she knelt down in the grass, and with tears streaming down her face, she surrendered. She was so tired and so hopeless. Life as she knew it was over. She closed her eyes, pressed her tear-stained face to the ground, and breathed out a very long exhale. She sank into the quiet and peace of Nature.

He found her early that afternoon. Calling her as he walked through the meadow, his heart told him something was wrong. A sense of foreboding grew as he neared their favorite brook. Carefully, he stepped through the grass, examining every flower petal as he looked for her. He found her lying in the grass, sun still warming her lifeless body. With a cry of anguish, he lifted her into his palm, hardly able to breathe.

Taking her limp, delicate body in his hands, tears coursed down his face. Shaking so hard he could barely walk, he stumbled blindly through his tear-blurred vision in circles before stopping and laying her fragile, lifeless body softly back on the grass.

Pulling up every bit of courage he had, he asked the Universe for help. He asked for grace to heal them both. He lay down beside her, miserable, lost, full of heaviness and finally accepting the responsibility for the sorrow he had caused her. Suddenly a voice whispered his name, making him shiver. He heard quite distinctly, "You are not to blame."

"How can I *not* be blamed?" he cried. "Look what I have done! It was I who hurt her, who broke her heart. She lies there lifeless because of me!"

"No," the voice replied. "You have given her a gift."

"Explain yourself!" he demanded, now angry that the voice was not acknowledging the truth, and even angrier that he could not see who was speaking to him.

"You cannot see the larger picture because of your belief system," the voice responded to his furious demand. "You must surrender what you think is real and work to accept others' perspectives of reality. It was from a place of openness that you were able to see and speak with the fairy to begin with. Now you only think about the past, and the past has no relevance. It simply carried you to where you are now, but beyond that it is not important. Stop wishing for things to be as they were and explore the experience you are having *now*. Experiences are not to be judged; they are only a means of transporting you from one point to another, and the only value they have is to find new ways to see and respond to life. They have no value beyond that. You drew a fairy into your present to help you grow, not for you to change her. She, in turn, grows from how she responds to what is happening to her. In learning from the experience you are having now, you will find the gift of which I am speaking."

"How am I supposed to believe you?" he demanded.

"Let go of your beliefs about this experience and the emotions that reinforce what you think, and a greater truth will be revealed," said the voice.

His anger burst into a torrent of tears, and he surrendered, sobbing, "I don't know anything."

"That's a good place to start," the voice said, "but actually, you do know quite a bit, things you remember from before your experience here on Earth. Things that you seem to have forgotten actually live on the edge of your memory. These things have guided you to live a life of *Ahimsa*...you know... 'Do No Harm.' You know this deep within you, for it is true."

"Where has that gotten me?" he wailed, tears racing down his checks. "I have nothing, I seem to know nothing, and I have harmed the one I value most."

"That's the wrong path you are taking, but I see how you feel," the voice said.

"NO, YOU DON'T!" he yelled. "If you understood, if you had a heart, you would help me, you would tell me what to do! If you had a heart, you would have compassion and fix this!"

"Actually," the voice spoke quietly, "I *do* have a heart. All beings who come to help on this planet arrive from love and light. Ours are not human hearts, like yours, but we do have feelings, and we experience great frustration when you ask for help, we appear, and *you* can neither hear us, see us, feel us, or understand our messages because of your own thoughts or beliefs. Even when you quiet your mind, you have such ideas about how we *should* appear that you do not recognize us all around you. Talk about frustrating! *We* wait for you to remove your blinders while you complain about not being helped! We are waiting for you to re-remember. And it is not up to us to fix what manifests from your choices; you must fix it yourself."

Sensing a shift in the light, he looked up from his tears and saw that the voice now had a form he could almost perceive. As his vision slowly shifted, he realized he could see a rather large being standing in front of him, surrounded by light. He was looking at an angel!

Now the angel said, "A few moments ago I explained to you that you have given the fairy a gift in the experience you shared."

"I don't know how to fix this, and I can't see a gift," he responded.

"This tiny being lying here is bigger than she allows herself to be," said the angel. "She only knows the joy of her experiences in Nature. She met you and discovered the enormity of the energy of love. But she is trapped in her own thoughts and ideas about what it means to love and be loved. You have not broken her heart, although she and you both *think* that is the truth. What you have done is broken through what keeps her trapped, so that she can grow into the fullness of *who* she is. Without your angry responses to what she says and does, she would have continued along her path, missing much of what is possible. She is *not* dead; she is deeply asleep. And in her sleep, she will dream her way back to you. She always does. She will re-remember the larger truth. You will be privileged to see a birth as she breaks into her Future Self, because you and she together have pushed the limits of what is possible to achieve together. And she will be privileged to watch your own birth into *your* Future Self, too. You must allow yourselves to grow through this experience you are having together."

"That's hard, *really* hard to believe, when I see her lying there because of me," he moaned. A new stream of tears began. Shaking, broken now, he asked, "How can I trust what you say?"

"Ah," the voice spoke. "Trust starts by accepting that you are divine and connected to the divine truth of Source. Even your mistakes have divine purpose. Trust starts by letting go of your stuck ideas about how things *should* be and what you think is right. Learn to trust what you are re-remembering. That opens the way for you to remember how to trust everything, including what I am telling you. It also shows you how to change (or fix) the situation."

"You must accept *all* of yourself, even when you are suffering from poor choices and actions. You must understand that within each choice was something you needed to progress in your wisdom, and at each choice point you actually did the only thing you knew how to do in that moment. It is only when you look back that you judge your choices as mistakes. Think about the word 'mistake.' It refers to a path, or a choice if you like, that you 'take.' When you discover that path or choice is wrong, you know you have 'missed' something, creating a 'miss-take.' If you wind up somewhere you don't want to be, recognize it, *love yourself anyway*, and make a new choice. You can't trust or love anyone or anything else if you don't learn to trust and love yourself first."

The angel continued, "All of what I say is true, but I know you won't believe it until you experience it for yourself. That seems to be the way humans learn. I *know* you don't care for advice, but this *is* important, and you *did* ask for help. I've been waiting a *very* long time for you to be able to receive what I can give you! Here is my advice: Take every experience as it happens, and then let it go. Building upon experiences from the past creates a pattern that you may not wish to continue. That's called *history*. You can look at the world around you and see 'history repeating itself,' which is simply patterns that have been repeated and accepted until they become solid. Those patterns keep you from responding freshly and fully to each new experience so that you can learn on your journey. Every moment is different; you cannot rely upon previous experiences to guide you about what is happening in *this* moment. Accept the choices you make, knowing that each one helps you grow. You can always change your mind and move in a different direction."

He started to respond but realized the angel was suddenly gone—or at least he could neither hear nor see it any longer. Exhausted from this exchange, he sunk into a deep and dreamless sleep in the grass beside the fairy, but not before he turned to her and said, "I'm sorry. I love you."

The angel was there again when he awoke, but he did not see it. He turned towards the fairy lying quietly beside him. As he gazed at her still body, he heard the angel say, "Don't be afraid. All is not as it seems. Come. Walk with me. She will still be here when you return, and you may find something nice to give her while we walk together."

Reluctantly he agreed, following the energy and the voice of the angel, miffed that once again he could not see it. "Why don't you make yourself visible all the time, so I can see you?!" he asked and accused all at once.

The angel spoke with quiet gentleness, "You can see me. You just have to remove the blinders of what you expect to see. You did that earlier. But now you think that I should appear in some fashion that makes sense to you. If you let go of your old perceptions and soften your gaze, you will perceive light and patterns of energy waves around you. Feel with your eyes. You may see them as colors, waves of energy, or misty shapes. I am here, and I am available for you to gaze upon, but you keep yourself from seeing me because of your unmet expectations and your anger. The kind of sight you are seeking comes from a place of surrendered heart—a place of trust. When you demand or threaten because you think it *should* be a certain way, you miss what is right in front of you. That is part of the challenge you have been facing in order to grow."

"Humph" he grumbled. But he was thankful for the conversation, so he decided not to tell the angel what he was *really* thinking. He had believed in other dimensions all of his life and had been very open to seeing whatever was present. He had always given love and light to others as service. Because he had lived this way and with his elevated comprehension about the world, he believed he had earned the right to see into the higher realms. He was angry now that he had been denied what he felt was rightfully his.

The angel read his thoughts anyway. "Yes, you have provided service, but you still believe that certain things are only possible in specific circumstances, which you are not in control of or clear about. You think that you have been forced to wait a lifetime to participate in other realms—too long for someone such as you who is willing to serve. Yet here you are in a relationship with a fairy! You think that you should be able to demand and receive what you believe to be just or fair.

"You are not willing to accept the idea that we *are* making ourselves visible, that we *are* helping you, or that you *can* see us. Your sight needs to be adjusted, along with your beliefs. The energies here now do not fit your old concepts. Have you noticed that the clouds are different? Have you noticed the moon is not always in the place it belongs in the sky? Have you noticed the weather patterns are strange? Have you noticed that when you travel, there are less road signs and that the maps are inaccurate? That is a clue for you. *There are no maps for the time in which you are living.* The sooner you stop relying on history and old belief systems (old maps), the sooner you will be able to see beyond what you think is real. Then you will see me and others whenever you wish."

"Why is this happening?" he asked the angel, catching a shimmer of light at the corner of his eye.

The angel responded, "Let me show you how to answer your own question: As a child you experienced some magical circumstances where you could accomplish certain things that felt normal to you, but others seemed to think they were unusual. You were able to do this because you remembered what was possible. You also met other-worldly beings, did you not?"

"Yes. I remember. Those experiences have always been special to me," he said.

"But now you have forgotten how to access your power from other dimensions because you have been trained to focus only on what you experience here in this dimension."

Tears welled up in his eyes again.

"Peace," said the angel. "Everything is as it should be."

He chose not to argue, accepting the gift of this remarkable conversation. "Please, Angel, or whatever you are, please tell me what happened? If I was once able to do special things, why am I so lost now?" He felt a soft pressure on his shoulder, a warmth that extended from the lightest touch into his heart, and his sadness lessened.

"Listen," said the angel. "This is very hard to understand because you have learned that everything has a specific cause and a definable effect, and that one thing follows another. That is true to an extent, but it does not occur exactly as you have been taught. Try to surrender to what seems outrageous to your perception. Let go of your conceptions long enough to consider that something else might be possible and true."

"Ok, I'll try," he agreed.

"Don't try," said the angel. "Do it!"

He nodded. "I'm ready to listen. Please help me to understand. Tell me what I need to know."

The angel began again, "The things you experienced as a child were clues. They were pieces of recollection to help you remember who you are (your divinity), where you came from, and why you are here. They were also pieces of remembrance to help you re-remember your Future Self. You have always known that you were moving towards a Future Self that was greater than what you have been for your whole life."

"Yes," he confessed, "I have always hoped that I could develop into whatever that Future part of me, the grander part of me, could be."

"The problem," said the angel, "is two-fold. First, you already *are* your Future Self. You just have to re-remember who you have always been and integrate all the pieces of yourself. You think your divinity is somewhere outside of you, something disconnected that you have lost. The problem is not that you have lost it; you have just misplaced it because you are not able to do what you know in your heart is possible. You are so angry that you cannot feel the love that is always there. Remember, all of you is divine, and until you can trust and love all of yourself, you cannot fully connect with your Future Self. You must love yourself every day, even when you feel miserable, even when you feel conspired against, even when you feel that you can't do anything right. Love yourself *anyway*, as you would an innocent child or animal. This way of living helps you to accept others unconditionally. That's really hard because you have incorporated all of your judgments about good and bad from all your parallel lifetimes into your actions here and now in this dimension. You think that it has to be a certain way and that your journey towards your Future Self is a linear progression, with each lesson learned helping create you into a better, lighter person. But evolution is not linear. It spirals as one experience builds on top of another."

There was the briefest of pauses, and then the angel continued, "That brings me to the second part. Pay attention. This is even harder to understand. All of your lifetimes (and you have many, for you are an old soul) are leading to the work you are doing now in this lifetime—integration. All of those lifetimes are occurring simultaneously, which is why I tell you that evolution is not linear. These other lives are parallel lives. Your work is to integrate all aspects of yourself in all dimensions here, now, in this lifetime that you are experiencing.

"You thought your 'work' would be to teach or heal others and that you would be someone that others came to for help or for greater understanding. That is an evolutionary step that many humans go through—holding the desire to teach or heal someone *else*. But every human has the ability to heal; it becomes available to you as you awaken and remember who you are. However, each of you is here to heal yourself, not to heal others! You are here to remember who you are, not to teach others! Your work right now is about cleaning up all the emotional misunderstandings from multiple parallel lifetimes, causing beliefs that are limited and have nothing to do with who you really are. Your emotions bring dysfunctional beliefs to the surface so that you can correct your perspective and stop making the same mistakes over and over. When you do not use your emotional signals properly to change your perspective, you have the same conversations over and over, even though they don't help. What you don't understand is that *every time you do this*, you put more energy into an old pattern that doesn't work. You simply must learn to respond differently in the *now*.

"One reason it is so painful—which seems terribly inappropriate to you after all the spiritual work you have done—is because your world is nearing the Big Shift. In other words, your planet is preparing to ascend into a new form. In these energies, if you want your outer environment to change, *you* have to change on the inside first. You and the others like you who have yearned for a better world for so long are struggling right now, stuck in old behaviors that do not serve you and that continue to cause you pain. When humans have experienced enough pain (and yes, I know you think 'enough' was reached some time ago) to learn how pain guides you to make changes, you will surrender your belief systems, let go of how you think things work, and say the magic words, *'Tell me what I need to know now.'* We have been waiting on humanity to reach this place for a very long time. You have to ask, and ask, and ask every day, surrendering over and over to possibilities, and living from a place of trust and peace. Trust and reflection will change you enough that you will begin to merge with your Future Self, in alignment with the planet's own path of ascension—the Big Shift."

"Why is it, Angel, that all the work I have done in my life does not help me now? Why should I keep asking when nobody is reaching out to help me?" he said, dropping his head in sadness.

"You mean when you *perceive* that nobody is helping you. What you perceive and what is real are two very different things. Just because you cannot see, feel, or touch those from other realms does not mean that they are not helping you! Just because you don't feel better and your life isn't working the way you think it should, does not mean you are not getting help. Part of the reason your life appears not to be working is because the old paradigm is dying, and the new one is not here yet. There are no more maps. Your only guidance is your intuition, which tells you that you are making a positive choice, and your emotions, which tell you that you need to reconsider your perspective.

"The fact that you have a relationship with a fairy proves that everything is changing! Model yourself after the deer who live fully in each moment and respond to circumstances as they arise; they are not concerned about the past or about what is going to happen next. Live every day from a place of acceptance without worrying about tomorrow. But most of all, trust and love yourself. Always trust and love yourself. If you do that alone, your perceptions will change, and those with whom you wish to communicate will be available for you to see and hear."

"I don't know how to do that. I am lost," he lamented, feeling sorry for himself.

"Listen," came the voice again, and he knew the angel was still with him. "You need to understand emotions, thoughts, and intentions. Emotions arise to show you how you are out of balance in your perspective or your actions; they act as signals to stir things up within you to promote change— not change outside of you, but within you. You make these changes by unwinding your thoughts. Intentions, which can be either conscious or unconscious, create reality, and they do so more quickly when they are coupled with strong emotion. As you change your thinking and your perspective or the way you react to circumstances, you can set clear and positive intentions for a more agreeable experience. Unconscious intentions, however, especially if coupled with uncontrolled emotions, create confusion and often injury. When someone says, 'I never intended that to happen,' there is

always an unconscious misunderstood intention
that created that reality.

"Often the conscious intention is to express
what one is feeling so that a reasonable change can
occur in the outer situation. But an unconscious
misunderstood intention lying underneath to have
someone else (or the Universe) take care of what
you are feeling or change the situation so you do
not suffer creates a different reality, especially if
coupled with unbridled emotional release. Emotions
released with this kind of unconscious intention
impair your own growth and cause harm to other
persons or situations, often creating distance and
separation between people when what you consciously wish is harmony. The intention for positive
change is not well directed in such cases, and
unintended realities are created. Paying attention
to emotional signals is important and necessary, for
those emotions show you that it is you who is out
of balance by either thinking incorrect thoughts or
dysfunctional beliefs or clinging to old wounds that
need to be healed and released.

"Until you learn how to use your emotions with
compassion, you set unconscious intention after
intention to repeat unpleasant experiences. Such

unconscious patterns enhance dysfunctional beliefs, of course. When you 'try' and it doesn't seem to work, if you think *'no matter how I try, it never works'* you set the intention for repeated failure. The Universe will continue to bring you situations that trigger your emotional reactions again and again because this is your *opportunity* to change what is out of balance within yourself. You have to consciously change your thoughts to do that.

"When you finally move through an intense emotion and realize that your reactions and thoughts reflect a perspective that is *not* true, you move closer to your Future Self. But you cannot do it only once or twice. You must start a new pattern within you by choosing to set conscious intentions in *every* moment, no matter what the Universe brings you. When you continue to tell yourself that you are powerless to change anything, you will continue setting intentions that create situations where you are powerless to change anything. That is the reality that you are creating. Your *power* is your *belief system* and the *choices* you make of how to respond in every moment."

Careful to be sure that what was being shared was being received and integrated, the angel continued, "Catch yourself when you become emotionally upset and examine your thoughts! Just breathe. Allow possibility. Choose your thoughts consciously. Humans do not yet understand the full power you possess for creating your own reality. In the midst of emotional turmoil, you forget your divinity and your powers of creation. Be compassionate with yourself, realizing that as *you* change, you will draw to you more of the peace and harmony you seek."

He took a deep breath, and asked, "How am I supposed to begin?"

The angel replied softly, "There is no beginning; there is only now. Drop everything you think about how things used to be or what works. TRUST! What I tell you works, just not in the way you may think.

"You have a few more years of this opportunity to change and grow, creating a harmonious experience through your conscious intentions. As I told you, this planet is changing in preparation to ascend into a new form. Humanity has the choice to change and evolve with it, or to go somewhere else to continue old karmic patterns of learning when this planet ascends. The choice, as always, is yours," the angel said. "Your experience here is and always has been an opportunity for you to expand your own awareness and evolve into a higher state of being in the Cosmos. The opportunity can be squandered as so many around you do, or it can be used to grow.

"It is no coincidence that you and the fairy found each other now. You promised each other long ago to come here and do this together. Now is your opportunity. Use it," the angel continued. "Put away your resentment, your grief, your anger, and your frustration. Live through each emotion, watching and correcting your thoughts, and then change them as you begin to realize that you can see other possibilities. The fairy is right about one thing: Love *is* the answer and the way to all you have ever wanted. I suggest that you love *everything*, even the hard times, but first of all love yourself. When you begin to do this fully, you will regain what you have lost. Realize that your judgments are simply a reflection of your lack of acceptance. They are not real. They come from your beliefs, and you can change them at any time.

"I have two more points to share with you," the angel said. "First, the truth has nothing to do with whether you believe it or not. It just *is*. Truth cannot be successfully resisted or denied, and truth is becoming more obvious now. The easiest way for you to make a transition from the way things *were* to the way things *will be* is to look at everything that no longer works and accept that there is a reason it no longer works, rather than judging it. This is facing the truth. Be curious about what comes next. Right now, you have been getting angry because things don't work the way *you* think they should.

Second, humans want to be in control. Your Future Self understands there is no control; everything flows as it should. Trying to control events is a function of time, and time is coming to an end. There will also be an end of control as time stops—things you control and the control of others over you."

The angel paused, waiting for the new realizations to be accepted, then continued, "The present is the only thing that is *real*. If your current moment is painful or hard and you focus on what is good, *even* while feeling that pain, you nurture the seed, and the possibility for more goodness grows. Some call this gratefulness. Some call it love. I call it *discipline*— Choosing the Best Thought, for as I have said,

THOUGHTS create

INTENTIONS that create

REALITY.

I cannot stress enough how important that is. It is THE LAW OF CREATIVE MANIFESTATION.

"You must manage your thoughts to create a better reality. And love can change anything."

This time he did speak up. "I don't think the fairy's love can cure what is wrong with me or change what I am feeling!" he protested.

Patiently the angel said, "I'm not talking about her love. I'm talking about *your own* love and your power to change what you believe. You deny your own power by *believing* that you are powerless. While you may not be able to change what happens in the world, you have the power to change how you respond to it, and that simple change will help you to experience more peace and acceptance. I know that much of what I have said today you will reject, because it does not fit with your current beliefs. But before I leave, I remind you that the more you open your heart to possibilities, the more you can bring forth the miracle you have asked for in your own life. Please remember your words, *'Help me!'*

"I am helping you to realize that you have a choice. You can discard all this as merely a dream and go back to the pain of your life, or you can open your heart to the possibility that what I have said is true and find your own intentions providing the miracle for which you have asked."

The meadow light was growing brighter; birds were chirping joyfully, and everything seemed more alive. He realized he had not been able to enjoy the simple pleasures of Nature for a very long time. Silently he thanked the Universe for his connection to Nature, something that had always been a part of him.

He turned towards the angel, who continued, "These new ideas may be challenging for you to understand. But every challenge gives you the opportunity to remember the truth. Set aside your judgments about yourself, others, and the world, and trust that everything is unfolding as it should. Make conscious choices moment-by-moment. Your Future Self, who you *really* are, has understanding and power, where your current personality has neither. Bend time a little bit as you know how by going into Nature or meditating. These are ways of dispensing with time so that you can connect with your Future Self."

He stood, thinking deeply about what the angel had shared. Then his thoughts of the fairy broke through his reverie about his Future Self. He wondered how he was going to create enough magic to bring her back to life and to restore what they had lost.

Reading his thoughts, the angel said, "I told you it is not as it seems. Take a gift from your heart to the fairy, something special to you both, and step beyond what you believe is true. *Trust* that she is well and happy. *Believe* you can make a difference. *Trust* that what you have to offer matters.

"Look around you," said the angel, "and see if you can find a present for her. And by the way, she has a name: Yewanerapna. When you give her your present, call her by her real name. It will awaken her."

There was a pause, and the meadow air filled with the familiar fragrance of Stargazer Lilies, which were growing close to where he and the angel were talking. As he breathed in the sweet fragrance, his heart opened, and suddenly, anything seemed possible. The Stargazers were all in bloom, calling him to pick them. He thanked the angel beside him and silently said thank you to the flowers. His anger was gone, and in its place grew a long-forgotten feeling of trust moving through every cell of his body. For a long time, he stood there as if in the deepest of meditations, trusting that everything would be okay when he returned to the side of the fairy with the present of the Stargazers.

Silence filled the air, and for a moment, he both felt and saw the bright light of the angel standing before him. Suddenly something within him shifted, and peace once again flooded his heart. "Thank you," he said.

"You are welcome," said the angel. "Thank you for really listening, and for beginning to build your foundation on trust. From here, you will evolve into the Future Self that is calling you. I am never too far away to hear your call and come to give you assistance. But for now, I am going to leave you to decide how to proceed, for the rest of your existence depends upon your choices. Time is short. Decide well. Breathe in the fragrance of these beautiful flowers. Take some of them to Yewanerapna. She knows the beauty of this place, for it was here that you first met. Take this gift to her, call her by her name, and she will awaken." And with that the angel was gone.

He gathered an armful of Stargazers and made his way back to where the fairy lay in the meadow.

Yewanerapna awakened to the wonderful smell of Stargazers and opened her eyes. The first thing she saw was the love beaming from his face as he lay beside her, propped on one elbow, watching her. In fact, he was surrounded by light! Her heart leapt towards his, and she met his outstretched hand. Something had happened though, not only to him, but also to her. Her body was now the same size as his; she was no longer the tiny being who could snuggle into the palm of his hand! Running her hands down her body with wonder, she said, "I don't understand what has happened to me."

He pulled her close, calling her by her real name, and she melted into him, a delicious sensation she remembered from somewhere else, a long, long time ago.

He smiled at her and handed her the Stargazers. "These are for you," he said, "a symbol of my love for you. I can't explain how you shifted in size, for I had my eyes closed, thinking and intending that you come back to me, alive and happy. When I opened my eyes, you were no longer a fairy, but a beautiful woman. I think my intentions for us to have a happy life brought you back to me in this form. I'm so sorry for all the pain I caused you. I didn't realize how I was hurting you," he said softly.

"But I had a wonderful conversation with an angel who helped me. I have much to share with you, but first, are you hungry or thirsty?"

She said no, snuggling more deeply into his embrace, enjoying the fact that they were matched now in size. It was perfect. Smiling at him, she said, "All I need is you. Please tell me what you learned."

And so he did. He explained about beliefs and thoughts and intentions that create reality. He explained about parallel lives and that real love had brought them together again and again, but their expectations and beliefs had torn them apart. He had become angry; she had become sad. He went on to share what the angel had told him about creating and stepping into their Future Selves.

"Basically," he said, "you and I recognized the *truth of who we are* through our very great love in spite of how we saw each other. But the shadows of what we used to believe or what we thought was true in this and other lives held us back from being our true selves. I believed I could not have what I wanted because everything was changing, and it often seemed that nothing I did made a difference. I got angry. You, it seems, became sad, believing that you would die without my appreciation of you."

She nodded, taking it all in. It felt right. "So I was feeling hurt because of my own expectations about our relationship," she responded. "I needed to change my perspectives to allow you to experience your own emotional guidance, without taking it personally. What I was feeling about you wasn't about you at all; it was about me!" A new light of comprehension sprang from her eyes. "And I didn't die, but a part of me that was out of balance died."

He looked at her for a moment, enjoying the beauty of her new form before continuing, "No, you didn't die. You only died to what you believed. We are changing into our Future Selves, the ones we remember from before we came to Earth. It is difficult and sometimes painful to let go of our old selves and step into our new selves, a birth process of sorts. But I am aware that birth is often challenging and painful. The way you have changed as you slept is only part of your movement towards your Future Self. We are making these enormous changes because there is a Big Shift coming in our world, and we must be ready."

Yewanerapna quietly said, "Everything that happened between us happened on purpose so that we could dislodge and dispel perspectives that no longer worked. And doing this is important now because there is a change coming to the planet. Is that right?"

"Yes, a Big Shift is coming," he said. "We can't hold on to old judgments, emotions, or wounds for our planet is shifting into the New Earth, and the energy of the New Earth will not allow it," he explained to her. "We have to work *very hard* to step into who we are becoming." He elaborated about how they only have a little while until the energies of love, joy, trust, and compassion would be present every day as time stopped.

She nodded and accepted everything he said as true, for in her heart she recognized that it was. The most interesting part to her was the stopping of time. She realized that part of her had always valued the present moment and ignored both the past and the future. It was part of her spontaneous nature. But she also knew that the emotions she had experienced came from either wishing something in the present was more like the past or wishing that it would be different in the future, without really experiencing what the present had to show her.

They lay there in silence for a long time, the light from the setting sun streaming over them and playing on their bodies. It was peaceful. Nothing more needed to be said.

After a very long silence, she asked, "And what are we to do until the Big Shift comes?"

"We are already in it," he explained. "It is happening now as we become lighter and lighter by discarding old beliefs and judgments. We must practice compassion and expand our perceptions by surrendering our beliefs, over and over and over," he said. "It won't be easy, but we will be together. That's very important to me."

She smiled and kissed him; it was their first kiss. "It is to me, too. In fact," she said, "Love is all that matters."

Looking deeply into her eyes, with one hand on his heart and one hand on hers, he asked, "Will you forgive me for the pain I caused?"

"There is nothing to forgive," she instantly replied, seeing the tears in his eyes. "I recognize that our experience helped us to grow." She smiled, her heart dancing in her chest.

Something shifted in the air. Quiet descended on the forest for a moment. They looked at each other, realizing that they were most fortunate to be together, on Earth, and in this beautiful place. They also realized that they were being watched, protected, and blessed. They were joining their lives together through their conscious intention. Suddenly the birds began to sing, announcing their support for a new beginning. It was time to begin living together in a more conscious and powerful way. They arose to begin their new life.

And so, through conscious intentions, they lived each moment of their lives as fully as they could. They had their challenges as things in the world fell apart, but they greeted each one with grace and compassion, following the instructions the angel had shared. Emotions came and went as belief systems disappeared, but they were ever true to their love. As time passed, hurtling towards its own demise, they learned that each moment was a new beginning, carrying them closer to their Future Selves. As they moved towards remembering who they truly were through each new realization, they lived happily with trust, ease, abundance, peace, and love.

The Tunnel of Truth

I have never been afraid of the truth. In fact, I consider myself to be an honest person. I am uncomfortable with exaggerations or stretching the truth, and lies are completely abhorrent to me. When others exaggerate the truth, use "acceptable white lies," or "forget" to tell me the whole story, I am disheartened. I always know that something is missing, but I cannot tell what it is.

But honesty is elusive where I live. Communication on Earth, my home planet, is a thing of expediency: people say what they feel is necessary at the moment, coloring it to fit the situation, and letting the rest unfold as it will. Concealing what one feels or thinks is a way of surviving on Earth. No one takes responsibility for how his or her words spoken in one moment will affect the next moment, or affect another person, which creates a continual sense of disconnection between people and a reliance on contextual truth rather than universal truth. This style of communication simply does not work for me. I feel alien, misunderstood, and alone. Others seemed to be more comfortable with lies and exaggerations than I am; therefore, I find communicating with others continually confusing, and I don't like it, even though I find myself occasionally slipping into the same patterns in an effort to fit in and be understood. But most often I find myself speaking directly from my heart, without the cultural overlay of choosing my words according to context or company, and causing myself continual challenges. For me, the truth is the truth, no matter where or to whom I am speaking.

As you can perhaps imagine, I am not popular. When people greet me, I see a varying array of emotions flash across their faces—from reluctance to dismay at the need to communicate with me at all. The words they choose do not match the tone of their voices, the smiles on their faces, or the look in their eyes. Sometimes they sigh, cast their eyes upwards, or give other little telltale signs that they really don't want to talk to me, even though they do their best to hide it. I am a problem. I can hear, see, and feel the existing deceit in almost every conversation, and I struggle because I do not belong.

People's thoughts move too fast today, having been trained to always get on to the next thing, rather than staying present with what is happening in the moment. Speed in the name of progress is an enemy to the truth that lives in the quiet moments when we could connect with our hearts and each other. Perhaps it is the pace of thinking that makes it seem impossible to communicate honestly and with depth. I prefer a slower pace that allows time for a clear and honest response at all times, where everything important can be appropriately shared. I see that way of being as a pathway towards living a life that is simple and deep. I don't know how I know, but I know that I have lived like this before—somewhere, sometime.

I am telling you this because even with my certainty that honesty is one of the most important things in life, I discovered that I was not being honest with myself. I learned that everyone on my planet, including me, was participating in an illusion of perpetual lies. This realization came from the experience I am about to share from a routine trip to Kepler 22b.

My job included travel to destinations where life was more harmonious and sustainable than what we currently experience on Earth. My specific assignment was to cultivate relationships with others who could benefit our own society on Earth. One of my favorite places to go was the outbase on Kepler 22b in the constellation Cygnus. I loved going to this planet because it reminded me of pictures I had seen of Earth before humans had stupidly destroyed their own environment and allowed technological Artificial Intelligence (AI) to take over the management of resources. Kepler 22b had tall trees with sunlight drifting through their branches, crystal clear streams in grassy meadows, mountains that were green in summer and covered with snow in the winter—things that no longer existed on Earth. Long before I was born, all the streams and rivers, all the trees, and all the sundrenched meadows were gone.

The Kepler inhabitants were a simple people, and I loved visiting them because their cooperative nature created a friendly and supportive environment that is very different from the complicated and competitive environment on Earth. Their expressions were genuine, and their simple smiles registered in their eyes matching their outstretched hands in greeting. And the landscape was—well, if not exactly like what I imagined Earth had been, it was still pleasing. The peach-colored sky held clouds of many colors, and they had large, deep basins of purplish water they called lakes, formed by rivers flowing from the mountains. Peering into such a lake brought feelings of calm and peace. People drank the water directly from the lakes and rivers, and it nourished them. On Earth, our water was pumped into our homes from underground, where it was collected from sewers full of chemicals and toxic waste, and then processed through a routine cleaning method that was ineffective in removing all noxious elements. We were given the proper antidotes to the poisons that remained in the water so that we could safely use it for bathing or washing our clothes. But no one drank the water; we didn't dare. We drank a variety of chemically formulated liquids that were designed to support brain activity, according to the latest science regulations. I sighed. Life was simpler and more honest on Kepler. There were trees unlike any I had seen in pictures from Earth. And there were creatures called birds, too, in various bright colors, each one singing a different melodic song. Yes, I very much enjoyed my opportunities to visit the Kepler people.

When it was time for my next routine visit to Kepler 22b, I smiled to myself and happily began preparations for the trip. Inside my craft, I set my course on autopilot and settled in for the journey. Gazing around the sterile environment of my ship, I longed for the strange beauty of Kepler that I would soon see. In the privacy of my craft, I could dress as I pleased, so I stripped off my standard daily uniform of a dull grey jumpsuit with the navy trim designating that I belonged to sector G-123. I pulled on a pair of jeans and a pastel silk shirt I had found in an antiquities shop. I always wore these clothes when I visited Kepler, for they were more in keeping with the environment there. Besides, these clothes gave me a different and happier image of myself.

My shuttle, made of glass and smooth metal, was purely functional with nothing soft or sensual anywhere to be seen. The stars, moons, and planets passing my porthole as I zipped through space were the only beauty available to me. My craft was equipped with the standard AI navigational unit and a replicator for all my physical needs. I turned to the replicator and programmed "Drink: Water" only to be met by the automated response, "No such drink exists." Settling with a sigh for the most neutral choice available from the standard chemical concoctions that were programmed, I turned my attention to my emotional needs. How I felt was my own concern, and I was not going to allow an automated replicator to program a falsely happy mood. I wasn't interested in altering my natural mood.

On this trip, I had determined to spend some quiet time examining why I was so unhappy. In terms of my physical well-being, I had everything I needed. I had a job that compensated me in standard units I could trade for various pleasures or necessities. I had modern, functional physical housing furnished with appliances that automatically provided for my needs and decorated with virtual photos of my favorite images—rocks, trees, water, and sunshine. I wished I could experience those things the way they used to exist on Earth, and it was part of my unhappiness that such a wish could never be fulfilled. I had a relationship with a very nice man. Our compatibility was so well matched that there was never any tension. In fact, I was bored in our relationship. There was neither tension to push against nor any challenges in the relationship to help me grow. Nobody on our planet was interested in growing or awakening into something more. That was something I definitely planned to explore within my own thoughts on this trip.

As I gazed out at the stars and the waves of cosmic rays I was passing in my craft, I found myself in a familiar place of tranquility—that place where my heart was at peace simply because my mind was silent. In this quiet place, I often found the answers I sought coming to me straight from my heart. I set my intention to simply receive what I needed and relaxed, letting go of all my concerns. It seemed strange to me that I was never able to easily access this place when I was on Earth, where there was so much psychic energy from so many people and everything seemed too artificial, too contrived, and too *fast*. Up here, time did not exist, and I moved through space without any need for measuring how long the trip was going to take. I would get there when I got there. Simple. Clear. Honest.

Suddenly I was jolted from my peaceful meditation by an extreme AI navigational adjustment. Glancing at the controls, I saw that we had veered quite unexpectedly and severely off course. As I looked out the porthole, I saw why. The craft was perilously close to a rather large piece of space junk. AI had performed the Debris Avoidance Maneuver (DAM), but it had not been extreme enough to correct an impending collision. AI simply did not have the experience required for predictability algorithms to work properly. In short, AI lacked the ability to make instant corrections based on judgment of current situations. I had that ability, but it was too late. I knew that the attempted maneuver would not clear us from the path of the debris, but I did not have time to make a manual correction. I could see the defunct satellite hurtling towards the craft at an alarming rate. But before I could gather my thoughts or even try to manually override the inadequate AI, everything went black.

When I regained consciousness, I suddenly found myself outside of the craft hurtling through space, disoriented, dizzy, and confused. My experience was compressed into a series of moments that I could barely assimilate. I didn't know where I was. I didn't know what was happening. I was tumbling through space at a rate that seemed neither fast nor slow. I just experienced moment after moment of confusion. It crossed my mind that I shouldn't have been able to breathe out here on my own, and yet, I was breathing—at least I thought I was. There was no struggle. I was just spinning in slow motion, moving towards a dimly lit object in front of me. My continual flips and turns prevented me from clearly seeing where I was going, but I knew that somehow, I had been thrust into a trajectory that appeared to have a definite goal.

And then I landed, if you can call it that. I was no longer spinning, and I felt a sort of solid form under my feet. I seemed to have somehow landed inside an enclosed space. As I fought to find my balance, I realized I was in a very narrow and dimly lit tunnel. I could see neither in front of me nor behind me because curving walls obliterated the view in both directions. How I landed here, I could not fathom. It was outside of all my training or even my imagination. Trying hard to think, I decided I must have landed inside part of some sort of old spaceship, and it must have been still somewhat operational, for I was still having no difficulty breathing. There was a slight incline where I stood. Without knowing what direction I should take, I struggled to stabilize myself and started walking up the incline. In the yellowish hue I could not see very far, but I could just make out that the narrow pathway curved and spiraled up ahead. It was impossible to see behind me, and the way forward was very unclear. Nevertheless, it seemed that there was no choice but to move forward; after all, on Earth, everything is based on forward progression, so I moved in the direction of my training—forward.

Rounding curve after curve, I began to find it more challenging to breathe. At the moment that I noticed I was struggling to breathe, I realized the reason—I was holding my breath; I was frightened. Remembering what my Pleiadian friends, Laarkmaa, had always told me about fear, I stopped to notice my thoughts and corrected them. There was no reason to be afraid. This experience was *different*, but it was not *bad.* I was lost, but I was not hurt. I had to find out where I was, and then I could determine what to do next. I looked around slowly in the soft, yellow light. Gradually my whole system began to normalize as I focused on the beating of my heart and the simple tasks of breathing and walking. One breath in. One breath out. One step at a time. With eyes and ears open and ready to perceive whatever was present without fear, I resumed walking through the tunnel.

I walked up the spiraling pathway in the yellow haze for what seemed like a long time. Then, suddenly, the tunnel became more narrow, and for the first time, I looked up beyond the enclosed sides. It seemed the walls reached forever, and I could see neither ceiling nor sky. Bringing my sight forward again, I noticed that the light was beginning to change. In fact, it was growing brighter. I blinked, adjusting my eyes, and I noticed that the walls were not just walls; they were mirrors. That was interesting! I could now clearly see myself and every movement I made. Yet the closer I peered into these mirrors, the more startled I became, for *these* mirrors were very unusual. They did not seem to reflect my reality. I could not reconcile who I believed myself to be with the image I saw reflected back to me. Yet it was definitely me, just not as I saw myself. The most obvious and startling difference was that the mirrors reflected that I was naked, while I knew I was not. I could feel clothes on my body. I slowly stroked the rough denim of my jeans and fingered the lace edge of the soft silk of my travel shirt. My outfit gave me a sense of optimism that beauty was still possible, even if it could only be found at the moment in old clothing. I touched the imitation pearl buttons on my blouse. They felt real. But in the mirror the buttons, the lace, the blouse, and the jeans were all absent. I was indeed naked. The more I stared, the more uncomfortable I became. It appeared that I was wearing absolutely nothing! My immediate reaction was to fold one arm over my breasts and extend the other in an attempt to cover my pelvic region, which I quickly discovered was impossible. The mirrors continued to reflect all of me. I could see every grimace on my face, the emotional reaction of every thought, and the bodily response to those feelings and thoughts as I subconsciously moved into various positions in a vain attempt to cover myself. Everything about me was suddenly transparent.

Again, I used Laarkmaa's guidance to treat this as simply a different experience and not label it as good or bad. I realized that this was a mystery I needed to solve; my only choice appeared to be to study myself in the mirrors. As I turned and looked at my reflection on both sides of me, my perceptions began to shift. I moved from my embarrassed self-awareness to simple curiosity about how I might appear to others. And amazingly, I began to see myself differently. As I gained insight after insight through that exercise, pieces of the mysterious puzzle began to fall into place. I recognized how the symbols of what I saw in the mirror were revealing information about my beliefs and my defenses about who I thought I was. I realized that my clothes did not hide me, nor did they make me more beautiful or desirable. My clothes only hid my nakedness from myself. Anyone with an open heart and eyes to see could see who I was, regardless of what I was wearing. My energy and my actions conveyed more of who I am than what I wore. I began to understand that these were Truth Mirrors, reflecting all of me in transparency, where every thought, every feeling, every bodily reaction was recorded and reflected back. These mirrors provided unadulterated *honesty*.

While I had experienced many, many "ah-ha" moments in my life on Earth and many levels of awakening and realization (in spite of the cultural disregard for self-discovery), never had I been able to see myself with such clarity. As I stared at myself in the mirrors, I felt embarrassed, ashamed, defenseless, and unsure of myself. But there was nothing to do but look and let those feelings move through me. The mirrors reflected me back to myself whether I walked forward, turned around, or stayed where I was. It seemed I was being forced to view everything that made me uncomfortable about who I thought I was. I began to look more closely at my reflection. I looked and looked. And I breathed and looked some more. Calming my busy mind and racing heart, I realized that there was no reason to be embarrassed or ashamed; I simply needed to accept all of who I was. There was nothing to defend because the only person attacking me was the part of me that judged myself. *This* was ultimate honesty. In that moment, I was clearly aware of just how much judgment exists on Earth and how I was being given the opportunity to completely release all judgment—of myself and of others—right now. I was in a Tunnel of Truth.

As my realizations unfolded, the light around me increased in brightness. As I relaxed and broadened my vision, I realized that in the brilliant light I could now see others in the tunnel just ahead of me. Strange. I had been certain I was alone when I landed here. I don't remember anyone else being hurled into space when I was. I don't remember seeing anyone around me as I struggled to find my balance, but here they were, others like me. I watched as they recoiled in reaction to the discovery of their nakedness; they hunched over or stooped down, turned around, and touched their clothes, perplexed at the dualistic experience. They seemed to be having the same or similar experiences of bewilderment and confusion about seeing themselves naked while they were actually clothed to my eyes. I could see both the clothed people and the reflections of their nakedness in the mirrors, and I realized that they could see me in the same way. Everyone was feeling embarrassment, shame, and a sense of being defenseless. Each one of us turned and crouched in an attempt to hide our naked bodies until we realized that our only choice was to accept what we saw reflected back to us. The reflections changed when we changed. With that realization I took in a deep breath, straightened my shoulders, and stood up straight. I smiled into the mirror, and I was astounded to see the mirror reflecting light from both my eyes and my heart. I was sending light through a simple smile! I tried it again after shifting my position and rearranging my face. I took in a breath, let it out, and smiled with every part of me. The light increased! And it was, indeed, flowing directly from my heart and my eyes.

Gradually everyone began to look away from the mirror and their own reflections, which no longer seemed important. Instead, we looked at each other, sharing smiles. I no longer cared whether I appeared naked or clothed to others; I was only aware of my need to smile and the connections I felt from smiling. Nor did I now notice or pay attention to whether others were naked or clothed; I only noticed their energy and if they were smiling or not. Slowly, every one of us in the tunnel were extending tentative smiles to each other, seeing the beauty of who we were as we shared light. As we did this, the tunnel became brighter and brighter!

Like stories I had read of a group of salmon swimming upstream or a flock of geese in flight, we began to turn simultaneously, one smiling body moving forward in unison. Some of us joined hands. Some of us walked alone, smiling at others. The tunnel began to widen into a path, and the incline lessened slightly. I glanced up, and for the first time I could actually see something other than the endless length of mirror extending into infinity. I saw colored light! It was far away, but it was there.

As we continued walking, the path widened even more, and slowly the walls reflecting our images dissolved. The feeling of being enclosed also changed; there was a sense of openness and expansiveness. Our bodies *felt* lighter, too. I seemed to be floating effortlessly while walking now, and there was no pain anywhere in my body. This feeling was astonishing, wonderful, delicious; it felt like I imagined falling in love would feel! It was like the remembered and familiar feeling of the sudden flush I felt on those rare occasions when I had felt seen and accepted, or maybe even loved. I remembered this feeling from somewhere. Although I had no idea how long I had been in the Tunnel of Truth, the magnitude of the experience made me think it had been days—well, in Earth time it may have been days. And yet, I was neither hungry, nor thirsty, nor tired. Everything seemed perfect, and I had all that I needed.

Suddenly the path stopped in the middle of a beautiful meadow that was almost indescribable. The air was incredibly crisp and clear, and I was breathing more easily than I ever had. An azure sea sparkled in the distance on the left and the meadow led to a crystal-clear stream on the right. There were gently rolling hills and rocks and trees and so much sunshine I could barely see the beauty of everything around me! And there were rainbows—multiples of them in the sky! I had seen pictures of Earth before we ruined the planet, and I recognized everything I dreamed of: the rocks, trees, water, sunshine, and rainbows. But I knew this wasn't Earth. We were somewhere else. This was a completely different place, or a parallel Earth of which I was privileged to be a part.

I watched people begin to intermingle, still smiling. We appeared to be a wave of people who had intended a better world so profoundly, that each of us had created a situation that brought us to the Tunnel of Truth where we could see how our beliefs had kept us separate, living in an illusion. My journey had been via a routine trip to Kepler 22b and a space crash. Perhaps I would hear the stories of others' journeys and how they arrived in the Tunnel of Truth, a portal to this new world.

As I smiled, I wondered, "Would Earth ever have been ruined if we had all been naked? If we had been responsible for every thought and every action because we were *completely* transparent, could we have saved Earth?"

The thought faded; it was no longer important. Earth was becoming a distant memory, and I was fully focused on and determined to respect the splendor of this beautiful place. I was here now, with others who seemed to understand the importance of honesty and transparency. A telepathic message floated through the air to each of us, explaining all we needed to know: "Here we live honestly, transparently, with kindness, compassion, love, and in Truth. Welcome."

It didn't matter who we had believed ourselves to be, where we came from, or how we got here. What mattered was the high vibration of our energy and our coming together in Unity through our intentions to manifest a better world. Everything behind us was just a story, just a string of experiences. I was home.

Parallel Love

Laarkmaa told her to think of what she was most afraid and work with it. She paused because it seemed she had already experienced everything that she was most afraid of, leaving her nothing to fear. Deciding that she should explore parallel lives to clear any residual trauma, she closed her eyes and entered into a life she had remembered as being most painful. Safe in Nature, with him by her side, she released her grip on the now and entered into the parallel life she most remembered. Slowly this reality faded away, and she found herself immersed in another place at another time, with him. In a dual state of consciousness, she asked her parallel self, "What are you most afraid of?" The answer came swiftly. She was most afraid of losing him, the one person in the world whom she deeply and completely loved and who loved her back.

As she pressed into the pain of those thoughts and feelings, the situation that needed healing began to reveal itself. He was gone. She had lost him— because it seemed he had lost himself and turned away from her and from life. She was now fully experiencing the parallel life.

The landscape of her entire existence had been one of almost unbearable extremes. "Almost" because she was still here. The journey with him had been full of vast expanses of desert where she thirsted for touch and he turned away from her nakedness. Or she found herself in an ocean of almost continual touch, connection, and gazes of appreciation. Crossing the border from one country to the other was often abrupt and full of extreme loss or need for adjustment (hers). She could bare her breast or reach to touch him, only to receive an unexpected withdrawal, with cutting remarks. Sometimes bitter, harsh words rained down on her and stung her heart when he was sufficiently unhappy. It seemed that he was the one who ruled the borders of when they connected and when they didn't. When they didn't, when they were in *that* country, she reached for the essence of him and found that she could not touch it, even in sleep.

Tonight was one of those nights. She reached and was met with a solid stone wall and a vast expanse of frozen tundra.

Moving further into the parallel life, she examined her thoughts. As her parallel self lay in the darkness, feeling quite alone, she thought about the question Laarkmaa had told her to consider: What did she fear most? During her life she had experienced betrayal, assault, accusations against her character, loss of fortune, loss of home, insatiable hunger, sickness, excruciating pain without relief, paralysis, and death (her own once, as well as the death of others), and most importantly, the loss of her cherished beloved. What else was there to fear in being human? Whatever experience came now could be no worse than what she had already experienced. Sighing into the darkness, she thought, "It's all just life." But in that parallel life, with her present consciousness, she knew there was a way to clear this old trauma.

The angels cried as they poured unconditional love upon her, realizing that with a simple change of perspective, there was no need for this kind of suffering. As they poured love into and around her, she felt something within her soften and relax. Now both her conscious self and her parallel self were moving and thinking in tandem. Slowing her breath, and quieting her mind, she began to slightly rock herself, a self-soothing technique she had learned as a child. Within minutes, she was asleep, dreaming a dream within this parallel experience.

But this time, with the conscious presence of her other self, her experience was different. Her dreams imprinted themselves upon her as she slept, her dreaming mind demanding that she pay attention to and remember what she was being given. Something unusual was happening. The landscape was shifting. And as she was forced to remember *everything* from this parallel life, she managed to master the depths of acceptance, which she immediately transferred into her current life. She realized that her task was to let go of the longing for things to be anything other than what they were and to be grateful for what she had experienced. She smiled in her sleep as her dreams replayed memories of her lying next to him with arms and legs entwined, breathing each other in as he murmured how much he loved her. She had had *that!* And now she realized she must release the longing for what was no longer. And from her deepest dreaming, she began to accept it. "Peace comes with acceptance," the angels whispered in her sleep.

Her dream this night worked some magic, and as she slept, her perspective in that life began to change. She realized she had traveled through this desert landscape periodically with him many, many times before, always longing for it to be as it used to be, and waiting, waiting, waiting for it to change again. This time would be different. Whatever the reasons that he was experiencing this pain and separation, she understood that her job was to walk compassionately beside him without wishing for things to be different than they were. Her subconscious awareness rose to the surface, and even in sleep in one reality, her conscious mind in the present reality realized that she was in school learning a lesson at deeper and deeper levels. When she wished for more, it caused a resistance and emphasized a sense of lack, for him and for her. He could read it on her face, in her body, and it probably increased his pain, too. The dream instilled the necessity for her to walk beside him in quiet acceptance and compassion. She was learning to experience a different kind of love. The angels made sure that this change of perspective, this subtle but necessary lesson of acceptance, settled deeply within her throughout all of her lives, even though she might forget parts of the dream the moment she awakened. As she slept and dreamed, she breathed out all the pain and misconceptions held in her heart that he did not love her anymore.

Time passed while she slumbered on. And then it seemed someone was gently rocking her. With a merging of her consciousness in both lives, she realized she had actually fallen asleep in this life, too. Part of her didn't want to awaken to the challenges she knew lay ahead, but the rocking continued. The other part of her remembered that she had intentionally entered a parallel life and cleared a very old and deep trauma. This part of her was eager to awaken with her new knowledge!

Slowly she opened her eyes and looked around. Having been actively in the other realm with a different set of circumstances, at first, she was disoriented. Sunshine was streaming down through a lacework of trees that arched over her, and she heard the tinkling of a creek nearby. How could that be? Hadn't she had gone to sleep in their bed? Everything was blurred. Gradually she began to sit up, feeling the soft, mossy ground beneath her.

Looking all around, her eyes finally came to rest on him. He was vibrant, healthy, real, and smiling. Without immediately remembering how they had come to be here, she looked at him. He was standing quietly nearby, smiling and holding out his hand. She struggled to her feet, still a bit dazed and feeling just a tiny bit sore. No, this was more than sore; she ached all over, some places more than others, as if she had done some very hard work or been in some great battle. But she managed to smile back at him and whispered, "Are you ok?"

"Oh, yes," he replied, still smiling. "You did it."

"Did what?" she asked with a puzzle in her voice.

"Remember the task Laarkmaa gave us? You crossed into another parallel reality to accomplish the task of correcting an imbalance that was making you unhappy and fearful here and now. Do you remember?"

"I remember the pain of seeing and feeling you withdraw from me after what seemed like years of harsh words and judgment. I remember aching from crying so hard. But that's not how we are now, so I'm not sure I can put this together just yet."

"What else do you remember?" he asked, encouraging her to dig more deeply into her memory.

Pausing, she reached back through what now seemed simultaneously like yesterday and a hundred years ago. She replied, "I remember loving you so much that none of it mattered. I remember that I knew the only thing that was real was our love, not what seemed to be happening to you or to us."

"What was your last thought as you remembered that life?" he asked softly.

"I remember summoning all of my courage and holding on to one single thought," she replied. "As all of the pain came rushing into my heart, my heart took control of my thoughts, and the last thing I remember was saying that I would not focus on your leaving me or what I had lost. I would focus on holding on to what I knew was real— on all that we had had together. The last words I remember were..." She paused, tears now running down her cheeks; then smiling through her tears, she looked directly at him and said, "I moved my thoughts away from the separation I was experiencing, and I remembered times of lying next to you, breathing each other in while you stroked me and whispered how much you loved me. Suddenly I was aware that I had no reason to be sad because I was so grateful for *everything* that we had shared.

All of it. You know, peace comes with acceptance. I released the longing for what was no longer. I had traveled through a desert landscape periodically with you many times in that life, always longing for it to be as it used to be, and always waiting for it to change. This time was different. I accepted that whatever the reason you were having that life experience of pain and separation, my job was to walk beside you without wishing for things to be different than they were and to do my own inner work. In that moment, it seemed like I had been learning that lesson at deeper and deeper levels for years, maybe even lifetimes. You know, when we wish for more, it causes a resistance and emphasizes a sense of lack, for you and for me. That's true for everyone. Being empathic, you could read my unhappiness on my face, in my body, and it probably made you feel worse, too. So, I determined to walk beside you in quiet acceptance and compassion. I learned to experience a different and more unconditional kind of love. Yes, I experienced pain, but I had also experienced unimaginable bliss and joy. The last words I remember were, 'I am so grateful, for I have had *that!*' And then I awakened to the life you and I share now, full of peace and happiness.

Reaching down to where she sat, he pulled her up and embraced her, stroking her hair. "You did it. You integrated that painful life with this one we are living together, and now you *remember.*" That's what an evolutionary journey is all about—remembering the deep and poignant lessons and integrating them into the now so that we spiral up to a higher vibrational level of being love. Most people think of having *past* lives where they have many different experiences. But they are not past, they are parallel, happening simultaneously.

"As we become more conscious and more aware of what we feel and think, we are able to cross timelines and dimensions to enter into other parallel lives as you just did where we can work out problems that are interfering with our sense of peace and balance or where we need to resolve something that is affecting us from another parallel life experience, like the one that brought you the sadness you could not explain. You see, we have different aspects of ourselves living out various stories or experiences in each of these lifetimes. Once we realize how to do this, we can leave the current circumstance temporarily to enter another dimension so that we can resolve the knots and problems that we create for ourselves."

"Yes," she immediately chimed in. "We have so many parallel lives, yet we only become aware of them when we begin to feel emotions related to particular circumstances that reflect problems existing in another dimension. Those emotions signaling imbalances can be so strong that they affect us where we are here and now, even if what we are feeling doesn't seem to make sense in our current situation. As we learn how to love across dimensions by stepping into other lives, we realize that wherever we place our attention, we can feel the emotions of that particular circumstance, and we resolve it, release it, and return to our current central life."

"And," he added," as you know and Laarkmaa has explained, in this lifetime, here, now, in this moment, we have the opportunity to integrate *all* of our parallel lives so that we are no longer missing parts of ourselves and so that we can feel complete as we remember and integrate all of who we are. It is a unique opportunity for humanity to evolve. After an experience of traveling into another dimension to clear out what you and I call karmic knots, we automatically change our perspectives about what we *believed* was true, and we accept a more encompassing reality where everything makes more sense here and now, too. This is the process of integrating all of who we are in the present moment. Experiences like the one you just had are important for helping us to access all of ourselves through each parallel life."

He smiled and kissed her. Then taking her hand, they began to walk down a lovely path in the woods with the stream beside them, tumbling over water-rounded rocks, and sunshine streaming down on them through the trees.

"You know, he said, smiling at her, "Something happened to me also. Do you want to hear about it?"

The What If Game

People had forgotten how to play the *What If* game, the game of imagining what might be possible. They were so accustomed to asking Google what would happen next, that they had eliminated their power of choice by forgetting their imagination. It all started when people shifted from using Internet for simple computer references for information, to relying upon Google to tell them the truth about everything in the world. More and more people began to see search engines as infallible, and soon Google became God. Those who fed the facts into the computer were free to alter those facts in any manner they chose, for no one was paying attention to what they were doing or what was happening. No one argued. No one contested the truth of Google's facts. After all, Gods are omnipotent and unquestionable. And so, as people relied more and more on Google to tell them what was true, they stopped playing the *What If* game. They simply accepted whatever Google said as undeniable fact.

Gradually, but quickly enough to overtake the beliefs of an entire species, Google began to alter the facts it fed everyone who asked questions. History changed. Facts changed. And the future became predictable. There was no place for imagination because everyone simply believed whatever Google provided. The people lost their power to create anything or imagine a new situation for themselves; they even lost the ability to think their own thoughts as their minds were increasingly owned and controlled by Google.

Stanley was perplexed. There was something niggling the back of his mind that was unsettling, to say the least. He had asked Google a question about women, but Google's answer didn't match what he saw and felt about Sara when they were together. Google proclaimed that women who laughed a great deal were not good prospects for marriage. But Sara's laughter raised Stanley's spirits and made him feel good. She never made fun of him or laughed *at* him; she laughed at the world and the silly choices people made when they reacted to situations and each other with drama and emotion rather than with the clear, light responses she applied to everything in her own life. Sara spent a minimum amount of time on Internet, just enough to meet the requirements of paying her bills. She refused to look up facts on search engines, preferring instead to rely on what she felt and experienced. She took long walks in Nature rather than spending hours looking up facts, seeking entertainment, or researching questions about life.

Sara was considered an atheist because she doubted if Google was real. She told Stanley that she believed Google was a virtual reality governed by someone else who fed false information into a machine to reinforce their own distorted world views. She dismissed Internet facts the same way she refused to engage in video games. "There is no *feeling* in those games," she said, and she couldn't get caught up in anything she didn't feel was real. Most people would say Sara wasn't real because she didn't participate in the things required by society. She was mostly self-sufficient, and she required little of the things most people acquired through Amazon, Google's most devoted partner and demi-god. She grew her own food, made her own clothes, and bartered her skills for the things she needed. She could cook. She could sew. She could calculate monetary sums for those who had forgotten how to add and subtract through their own dependence on technology. She could read and write for those whose eyesight was failing from too much computer use. She could listen and be a friend (although she did not charge for that). Most of all, Sara laughed, and people enjoyed having her around.

Somehow Sara's skills were always enough for her to get whatever she needed. But people who did not engage with Sara were frightened of her because she was so different. Even her kindness could not deter them from judging her as an atheist and trying to convert her to their way of thinking and believing so that they could feel more comfortable around her. They felt she threatened their way of being simply by being different.

Stanley first met Sara by chance, even though Google denied that chance existed. Google claimed everything in life was logical, explainable, and predictable. But Stanley could not explain his detour to work one morning or his surprisingly intuitive decision to stop and visit an elderly friend of his parents. His parents had been dead for over twenty years, and he had not seen Mr. Willoughby in at least ten years. Hoping he still lived in the same place, Stanley steered toward the unpaved road leading out of town. About twenty minutes later, he was parked in front of the old yellow house, its paint peeling, the door sagging, and the front window cracked. Cautiously, he got out of his vehicle and walked to the door, which was instantly opened by a young woman with a beautiful smile. She introduced herself as Sara and invited him in when he asked if Mr. Willoughby was home.

Ben Willoughby was delighted to see Stanley, although somewhat surprised by his sudden and unannounced visit. When Stanley explained that he had experienced a strong feeling that he should come by today, Ben Willoughby chuckled, and with a secret smile, nodded in understanding. Then he said simply, "It was Sara. She often does that."

"Does what?" Stanley asked, puzzled.

"Sends out smiles to people in need of one," Mr. Willoughby said knowingly.

This puzzled Stanley, but he didn't question Mr. Willoughby. Instead he chose to speak to Mr. Willoughby about how he was and what was different in his life since they had last been together.

Looking around the living room while waiting for Mr. Willoughby's response, Stanley could not see a computer anywhere. He silently wondered how he managed his life without one, and how Sara had come to be there with him.

When Stanley asked the last question, Mr. Willoughby simply said that a friend had recommended Sara to help out around the house, and she had been coming every day for three years now to help out.

Sara was now cutting vegetables in the kitchen in preparation of making a soup and salad, and when Mr. Willoughby asked Stanley to spend the morning catching up and stay for lunch, Stanley eagerly accepted. He excused himself long enough to call work and tell them that he would not be in today. He did not have to give a reason for his absence because he had 108 personal and sick days in his account. Stanley never got sick; he had no family; basically, he was simply a reliable worker all the time.

The meal was simple but delicious: soup and rainbow-colored steamed vegetables with hemp seed sprinkled on top. The atmosphere as they talked and ate was even more delicious, and Stanley realized that he had been hungry for this type of communication for a very long time. It was more nourishing than the food. He stayed longer than he had intended, soaking in the feelings of comfort, safety, camaraderie, honesty and transparency, and maybe even love. The atmosphere was so unconditionally supportive that he didn't want to leave! But at last, seeing that Mr. Willoughby was tiring, Stanley reluctantly pulled himself away, promising to return again very soon.

After that day, Stanley often wondered if Sara had added something extra in the soup. He was no longer able to stop questioning things that he had previously accepted as facts. He felt more alive, especially when he was with Sara (which had become a regular occurrence now) or when he was spending time in Nature. In fact, he was beginning to question if Google really had any idea how laughter made someone feel. In spite of Google's proclamation that women who laughed were not good candidates for marriage, Stanley had made up his mind. He was going to ask her to marry him. And now he knew what was niggling the back of his mind. He was remembering how to play the *What If* game.

"*What if* Sara said yes?"

"*What if* they lived their lives happily together from now on?"

"*What if* they had children who also laughed all the time?"

"*What if* they relied on Nature and each other instead of Google?"

Stanley was remembering the *What If* game, and he was going to play it for the rest of his life with all his heart.

Hotel Casa Tota

Cassie and Noah's trip to Baja to write a book on human evolution was more formidable than they could have ever envisioned. In short, *everything* went wrong. The house they agreed to care for in exchange for a place to write all summer was a disaster when they arrived, with broken windows, animal droppings everywhere, smears of grease all over the kitchen, no air conditioning, and broken pipes. The beds were too soft, and the linens were disgustingly dirty. It was a wretched beginning. Nothing was as it had been described or promised. Even the weather was unwelcoming, with heat so intense it took their breath. To relieve the shock of arriving to the catastrophe of their temporary new home, they decided to walk to the ocean, which was supposed to be just steps from the front door.

Picking their way through the droppings and broken glass to the terrace, they squinted into the bright sunlight, searching for the sea. Yes, it was steps to the ocean, but when they started walking they found there were 890 of them! Not as close as they had expected. There was a long stretch of almost deserted beach, but it ran at a steep angle from land to sea, making it difficult to walk on the beach. Nevertheless, they walked for about an hour, watching the waves crash upon the shore with such fierceness it alarmed them. As the sun began to set, they made their way back towards the house. Before walking up the path to the house, Cassie decided to brave the waves for a moment and waded into the edge of the water. She was immediately knocked to her knees in ankle deep water and sucked backwards as she struggled desperately to regain her balance. Noah ran to her rescue, pulling her from the grasp of the unseen force that threatened to take her away from him.

Their delight at being only steps from the ocean (even if there were 890 of them) turned into a terrifying nightmare as they realized just how violent the sea was outside their door. This ocean was *angry*. They quickly realized that their idea of walking on the beach and swimming in the ocean during writing breaks was a complete fantasy here in this place. Unlike other writing retreats at other oceans around the world, they knew that *this* ocean was not safe—it would kill them.

Food was also an issue. Cassie and Noah were vegetarians, and they had been told that vegetables were abundantly available in Todos Santos. That may have been true in another season, but during the summer the crops burned in the fields under the scorching sun, and restaurants closed or served only basics, which of course did not include the vegetables Cassie and Noah needed. Although they could find an occasional limp salad, for the most part they found themselves living on coconut milk and peanut butter.

In the intense heat of the next few days, Cassie and Noah worked furiously to turn the shattered house into a temporary home where they could do the writing they came to do. They were not going to be deterred by outer circumstances. Cassie stripped down to her halter-top and cutoff jeans and Noah worked without a shirt, sweat pouring down both of them in visible rivulets. They bought sheets and towels, new pots and pans, and hired someone to fix the pipes and the windows. Air conditioning, it seemed, was not an option, so they determined to simply use fans and adjust to the new climate since it was only for a few months. But as the days passed and they struggled to write in the sweltering heat, frustration and irritability began to creep into their conversations.

Nights were even worse than the days, if possible. They fought to find elusive sleep, the heat causing them to lie in pools of their own sweat. Often when they finally collapsed into exhausted slumber, they would be awakened by the stench of burning garbage in the air. Sputtering, choking, coughing, and unable to breathe, their consciousness jerked them into full awareness. No matter how tight they closed the widows and doors, that horrendous smell seeped in, burning their eyes, their throats, and their lungs. They found themselves being cross or short-tempered with each other, and of course, the writing dried up completely. There was no flow. They were stymied, stuck, and unable to produce a single coherent word.

Finally, after a month of intolerable agony, they decided to check into an air-conditioned hotel in town. At least they knew they could get a salad at the restaurant there, and they could finish the book they had come to write without the distracting and unbearable heat.

Hotel Casa Tota was clean, cool, refreshing, and the staff was unbelievably interested in Cassie and Noah and concerned about their comfort. They were greeted with smiles and genuine concerns about making their stay pleasant, both while they were in the restaurant and in the privacy of their own room. They quickly found that the staff would cater to their vegetarian diet smilingly, offering as many options as they could muster with no questions asked. They were even given discounts at every meal for being "special guests," and they were encouraged to stay for as long as they liked. Everyone on the staff from the owner, Miguel, to the front desk staff to restaurant waitpersons knew their names, how they liked their food, and what would make them most comfortable. When they walked into the restaurant, the music would change to their personal preference of tunes. Special treats were offered with smiles at each meal. In short, the entire experience began to feel slightly unreal because there was *absolutely nothing negative* in the people or the atmosphere.

In this environment their ability to write swiftly returned, and the words flowed with astonishing ease. The manuscript was finished and polished within a couple of weeks. Having fulfilled their task, Cassie and Noah decided to stay a little longer, just to enjoy the harmonious atmosphere and to restore themselves before leaving Todos Santos. They slept and ate in peaceful rhythms, and days passed without being counted as they watched the other guests come and go. While they often smiled as incoming guests arrived, they never seemed to see anyone check out, no matter what hour they were watching the reception desk from the birds-eye view of their balcony. People seemed to check in and then disappear. An old 1970's Eagles song *Hotel California* bubbled up, and Cassie found herself singing, "You can check out anytime you like, but you can never leave." However, nobody seemed to be checking out of Hotel Casa Tota; they simply disappeared. Something was strange, but Cassie and Noah couldn't figure out exactly what it was, so they ignored it, continuing to absorb the ambient atmosphere and care they were receiving. All they could see was the ever-present harmony around them.

Because Cassie and Noah both had very creative minds, keen observational skills, and intense curiosity, they began to wonder if this hotel was some kind of a portal, but they were unsure exactly where it might take people or where to look for it. They knew something was happening that they could not explain, but attributed it to their imagination. Most likely there was a perfectly logical explanation. After all, the staff at the hotel were all so kind, so courteous, and so accommodating. They all seemed to genuinely care for their comfort and were continually solicitous about what they could do to make their stay better. And yet, as pleasant as all of this felt, it *was* odd how people continued to disappear.

One night they were shocked to be awakened at the hotel with the stench of burning garbage. For two weeks, their nights had been free of this intolerable smell. Even more surprising, it seemed as if they were closer to the source of the burn than they had been at the house where they had been staying. Since they were both wide awake and completely unable to go back to sleep with the pungent smells assaulting them, they decided to investigate. Quickly they agreed to explore where the smell was coming from and see if they could find the source. After pulling on their clothes as they coughed and blinked back tears from their eyes, they made their way to the door. Once outside their room, the smell was so horrendous they almost turned back. But no, something told them it was time to search for the cause of this distressing smell, no matter what they might find. So they crept down the stairs of the hotel landing, following the smell and sounds that seemed to emanate from the back of the hotel. There was an alley there, and although it was completely cast in shadows, there was no doubt that they were going in the right direction, for the smoke got thicker and the smell more awful. Finally they emerged from the alley but remained standing in the shadows of the fire, where they could watch unseen.

What they saw horrified them! There was a huge bonfire, and there were people burning in the middle! No wonder the stench was so terrible; they were smelling the stench of burning human flesh! Who could be doing this, they wondered, and who were these people on fire?

Peering through and around the flames, they saw colorful waves of what appeared to be energy in human shapes on the other side, applauding and encouraging those in the fire. They listened for shrieks of agony or screams of anguish, but none were forthcoming. Instead, amazingly, they heard cries of liberation and exclamations of joy! What they saw, what they heard, and what they smelled were at odds with any consistent reality they had ever encountered. The contrast between sounds of delight and the dreadful smells was completely incompatible, and yet, there was no denying what they smelled or what they saw. Trying their best to put the pieces together to comprehend what was happening, they looked above the flames, and what they saw was beyond amazing.

It seemed that the people in the flames were releasing layers of themselves as the heat seared through them, and yet they themselves were not burned. What was being burned were the layers of beliefs and negative, fearful thoughts that had been layered so deeply within them that the density of those thoughts and beliefs trapped their spirits in the human forms to which they were accustomed. Cassie and Noah received this message in an astonishing instant of realization about what was occurring. Now, the people in the flames were—by choice it seemed—releasing those restrictive thoughts and beliefs that had held them in their current form, choosing to transform into something different, better, and freer. The awful and suffocating smell was the stench of negativity and fear that comprised all the judgment, blame, anger, jealousy, and hatred they had experienced in their lives. The fire was actually purifying the people who were standing in it, and they were becoming lighter and lighter, the flames searing away those no longer desired negative thoughts and fears. Layer after layer wafted up into the smoke, releasing the stink of judgment and fear as the people in the fire began to take on wavelike forms of light.

Cassie and Noah looked from the fire to the other side where the colorful energy forms were encouraging the people in the fire. Slowly, one after another, as the layers of negativity were burned away, people were emerging from the fire and moving to the other side. Only they didn't look human in the same way now. They were lighter and brighter. They looked more like the colorful wave shapes of energies on the other side of the fire, and they were embracing each other!

It didn't take Cassie and Noah long to put it together that the forms we humans assume to be normal on Earth are the forms that have built layer upon layer of negative thoughts, beliefs, fears, and emotions into the forms that humans now carry. The density of those thoughts gave humans a dense physical form and caused them to experience a sense of separation from each other and from everything light and good in the Universe. How lovely the emerging beings were as they came out of the fire, sparkling with crystal clear colors and light! How joyous and free they appeared to be!

Cassie and Noah had been working to raise human consciousness for their entire lives through the books they wrote, the lectures they offered, and with personal consultations. They were tired; they were frustrated; and often their hard work did not seem to make much difference when they looked around at the general state of humanity. They knew there was something larger and brighter waiting for them and for all humans who wished to be different and better. Recognizing that the fire would help them to release all their own negative and dense vibrations, thereby allowing them to transcend into a lighter vibratory form, they now fully comprehended the choice these people were making.

With a knowing look at each other, they stepped out of the shadows, joined their hands together, and ran toward their freedom into the fire.

The Great Change

"For the Yellow People,

Who saved my life by making a change."

The people were fractured. There was no other way to describe it. Granzo and Hashika had taken human forms themselves to observe the humans on Tehra for two months now. There was no coherence or consistency in the human's behavior. There was no sense of a unified purpose or striving for attainable goals of improvement. Even within small units (called families) Granzo and Hashika observed irregular patterns of behavior without reason or rationale. Most individuals within each unit performed with discord and conflict; they were loud, and they emitted waves of heated energy that was uncomfortable to be around. The majority of the

people Granzo and Hashika observed were completely fractured. Each member of these units
seemed to be concerned only with his or her own
needs or desires. The small ones squirmed, ran away,
and made loud, distressing sounds. There was no
handholding, but sometimes the larger members
would jerk an appendage of a smaller one to make
it comply, simultaneously using disturbing shrill or
booming sounds. In turn, those jerks and sounds
invoked even louder, and more distressing sounds
from the small ones, who continued to squirm
and try to escape the grip of large arms reaching to
restrain them. The large ones just jerked harder and
harder until the small ones submitted. Sometimes
the large beings even used violence, striking the ones
smaller than themselves. It was abhorrent behavior
and difficult to watch.

There were, however, some units that functioned
coherently and well, with each member doing
its part and the larger beings skillfully caring for
the smaller ones. These units had attained a kind
of flow where each of the larger ones knew what
was required and understood how to achieve it.
They worked together. The little ones did not make
those disturbing, loud noises so many other little

ones made, but instead they emitted delightful sounds of cheerfulness (called laughter) while the larger beings smiled and quietly communicated. There was eye contact and handholding, and these units (usually from two to six people) functioned in a way that was pleasant and somewhat predictable. But there were very few of these supremely functioning units.

Granzo and Hashika continued studying the people of planet Tehra. The people here seemed more concerned about how they appeared than about how they acted. They were discourteous to those around them, behaving as if they were entitled to whatever they wanted, rather than being grateful for what they already had. Their manner of dress, to Granzo and Hashika, was ridiculous, flashy, and ill designed for functionality. The clothes of the males seemed too large, while the clothes of the females sometimes fit so tightly that various body parts spilled out of the clothing, which surely must be uncomfortable. Certainly Granzo and Hashika were uncomfortable themselves in the costumes they were wearing to blend in. Even the footwear the females chose was questionable. Granzo and Hashika watched as the females balanced

themselves on high stalks on their feet that separated them from the ground and their ability to
feel the natural rhythms of their planet. They also
appeared to be obsessed with talking or recording
images of themselves in various poses on little
devices they carried with them.

Granzo and Hashika quickly ascertained that
one of the problems with these people was related
to these devices. They assessed that each human,
particularly in the dysfunctional units, seemed to
be addictively attached to a small technical device
that commanded all of their attention. These devices
appeared to put them in a hypnotic zone, where
they lost contact with others around them and
their environment. The addiction was so strong
that they resisted the need to place their attention
elsewhere and became irritable if forced to engage
with the outer world or with each other. Larger beings would ignore the smaller ones in favor
of the devices, which of course, provoked loud,
distressing noises from the smaller ones, who
needed their attention. Sometimes the larger
members provided technical devices for the
smaller members, too, which put the small ones in
a hypnotic zone for a while, but only for a while.

Eventually the small ones would become distracted by something in the external world or by a physical need and demand attention. The larger ones would try to jerk them back into submission once again to quiet them rather than caring for their needs.

As Granzo and Hashika looked on, they saw that most of the people had lost interest in Nature on Tehra, in each other, or in operating together in harmonious flow. It seemed all they were interested in was connecting through their little devices and recording images of themselves. They had become completely self-absorbed and selfish. Each one with a device wanted only whatever he or she wanted, regardless of how his or her behavior affected others. This attitude reflected in everything in their lives, whether they were shopping or driving or walking from one place to another. They even stopped—sometimes dangerously—to use their devices in the middle of the street in traffic to gain information. Or they would stop abruptly in doorways of stores or other public places to send or receive a message or to record images of themselves, causing others behind them to stumble, disrupting the flow of everyone around them. They seemed to view the images they recorded as their true selves, rather than recognizing that their essence actually radiated from the inside to the outside where others could see it. It seemed that their hearts were closed and as cold as the images they so ardently recorded. Granzo and Hashika took notes. It was very obvious that real communication or touch in this species was dying as it was replaced with the use of their digital technical devices. Granzo and Hashika even saw very small units of only two people, who each favored tapping on his or her device more than touching, looking into each other's eyes, or speaking directly to each other. There were no soft tones exchanged or knowing looks between them—just shrugs and separation.

Yes, the people were fractured.

It had been a thousand years since Granzo and Hashika had visited planet Tehra for observation. The last time they had been here they had witnessed vast waves of aggressive energy, and watched the strong taking from the weak, who had no choice but to either submit or fight back and die. There were great, bloody battles. The people of that time were afraid of and fought against anything that was different from themselves. The fierce sense of competition was palpable, erupting in violence and war all around.

A thousand years before that, their visit had revealed much of the same behaviors, with different tools and different practices used for the same end, although the clothing had been more functional and comfortable. When Granzo and Hashika had referenced the logbooks even further back, they had read comments about competitive behaviors masked as benevolence. In a place called Atlantis, the rich and powerful had convinced the citizens that the devices they produced for common use would bring more ease and harmony into their lives. It brought less. Some people protested and were killed, which seemed to be a common theme on Tehra. As the fascination with and dependence upon more and more advanced technology grew, the civilization of Atlantis had succumbed to the allure of their technical power at the expense of life, and the civilization had completely annihilated themselves and their land, as well as other lands around them. Only a few survivors on a neighboring (and more peaceful) continent had survived to continue the species.

It seemed the people of Tehra had learned nothing, for they continued to repeat the same patterns of dysfunctional and selfish behaviors. Now they were repeating the same choices as they had made in Atlantis, and Granzo and Hashika were concerned. The people's leaders were once again foisting devices upon the people as well as satellites in the sky that beamed deadly electromagnetic frequency rays into the planet, with empty promises of a better life, and the people readily accepted and believed their lies. In actuality, the leaders were building a type of Artificial Intelligence that Granzo and Hashika could see would eventually take over the precious gift of human choice. The radiation from this technology would also make the people and the animals very sick. It was already killing trees and plants. Yet the people were impatient to receive each new version of their devices, eagerly seeking them out and quickly engaging in the mesmerizing and ever-growing allure of an imaginary reality that superseded the beauty of Nature and the planet around them. The hypnotic devices being distributed to the people were indeed dangerous and addictive; they drew people away from an awareness of their immediate environment into a fascinating world of imaginary images on a digital screen. People were learning that they did not need to take responsibility for themselves (or how they affected others) because everything they needed or wanted was being supplied through their devices—not only information and the opportunity to present themselves in photographic poses, but also through the device's emitting of artificial tones that soothed them into a false stupor of non-thinking. They did not realize that by submitting to this continual use, they were giving away the power of their own choice.

The steps taken by leaders to convince the people that these devices represented progress followed the same pattern that had succeeded in luring people to their doom in Atlantis. The first devices gave ease and flow of information and communication and appeared to be controlled by the people who used them. By the next generation of use, the people had become addicted to the ease of obtaining whatever they wanted through the devices and were susceptible to subliminal messages that had been secretly added. By the third generation, they had forgotten how to use their own powers of intention and thought, and the freedom of choice was surrendered before they even knew what was happening. Now this pattern was happening on Tehra again, and again people were oblivious.

In Atlantis, the increased technology had caused such an imbalance that the entire continent had exploded. Today, the people's leaders were taking a more insidious approach, giving actual intelligence to each new generation of technology they created. The more advanced devices allowed surveillance of the population and were already linked to everything the people needed. Additionally, each piece of technology was linked to a larger intelligent unit that would allow the technological devices to communicate between themselves, without human programming. That piece of technology had not yet been revealed, but it was in place. The name for this technology was the Internet of Things, suggesting an intentional raising of the value of things over the value of people in importance.

For now, the people had intelligent refrigerators that recorded what was depleted in their stores of food and automatically ordered it again. They had appliances that automatically brewed their morning drink and provided toasted bread at a specified time (regardless of what time the humans may choose to awaken and begin their day.) They had machines that cleaned their houses and decided what was trash and what was not, according to where in the house it was placed. If a person dropped something by mistake, it was lost forever. They had transportation that automatically decided what route they would take and how fast they would travel when a destination was programmed into the machine. With that kind of intelligence, the devices themselves would soon enough be able to determine if the people were allowed to travel at all. It would not be long before the technology would overtake human choice, and once Artificial Intelligence was completely attained everything Granzo and Hashika's colleagues had worked so hard to achieve on this planet would be lost.

Granzo and Hashika sighed, looked at each other, and shook their heads. In a shared impulse, they shifted their forms to light and beamed themselves to their craft, leaving the clothing they had been wearing in a pile. They then shifted their energy again into their natural forms, donning their comfortable and beautiful robes. It was time to report to the Council. By all appearances, the experiment had failed. The question to be discussed at the Council meeting was not how (or even if) to save the planet and grant cosmic citizenship to all the people. The humans had already made that choice on their own, apparently unable to rise above their preferred disharmony, selfishness, and discord. They had become so ungrateful for the gift of life, so disconnected, and so complacent that they had chosen technology and Artificial Intelligence over peace, unity, flow, and respect for all life. The question now was about whether to intervene one more time for the benefit of just a few evolving people to re-introduce the higher principles that made it possible to achieve a more reasonable and meaningful existence before the collective of the species destroyed themselves and their planet. The Council knew they could not interfere with human choice—that was the law— but they could (and had many times) sent members to teach by example.

Granzo and Hashika thought that perhaps this was necessary *just once more* to demonstrate to the small enclaves of people who incorporated the higher values how to proceed. Would it make a difference? Could the higher vibrations of the few overcome the lower vibrations of the majority? Those few who worked in harmony, not only within their own small units, but also with other units were different. Hashika believed the question now should be what could be done to support the evolution of those who valued life, who did not fight among themselves, butcher animals, or treat others unkindly? They were suffering in their current circumstances. What was to become of those few who were distressed by the actions of their peers and their ancestors, those who could envision a better way to live, and who were trying to achieve it? Could *they* be saved, even if the others destroyed the planet? Even as she had this thought, she realized it was an unthinkable question, for it broke the law.

Nevertheless, these questions were in the forefront of Granzo and Hashika's minds as they made their report, although they knew that the Council was not prepared to make a decision that would resolve the issue only for those few who were different. They were prepared to discuss the question of whether one more demonstration would make a difference to the whole. They were convened to discuss, after hearing Granzo and Hashika's report, whether to abandon the experiment entirely, letting it play out to its logical conclusion, without their further guidance, or to enter the Tehra environment once again, setting examples of higher vibratory living for those who were willing to learn. Most of the elders felt this would not make a difference because the people were simply too fractured to heal and change. The elders had sent representatives no less than five times now to this planet. The people always managed to drift back to the same patterns of competition, greed, selfishness, separation, and disharmony. The question before them remained focused upon the possibility of one more intentional visit to demonstrate a better way to live.

The hall was filled with soft, lovely colors of the robes that flowed around each elder. As always, the colors worn were chosen for the energy that each member wished to connect with or express. Orbs of beautiful light circulated throughout the space, radiating peaceful and joyful vibrations. Today there was an atmosphere of electric intensity that presaged an important decision. Granzo and Hashika took deep breaths, stepped forward, gave their objective report and observations, and then quietly stepped back to be seated. They had done all they could. Now they sat and listened as the Council talked about the 5G and 6G satellites that were presently circulating around the planet for greater control of the people. They discussed the ill health effects and irradiation already present that the people would continue to endure as life died out. Moving away from the serious nature of the discussion, one Council member joked that the Artificial Intelligence being employed might actually in some ways be more harmonious in the Universe than the messy, emotional, and unpredictable mélange humanity had become. But he was not serious, and the other members completely disregarded his poorly chosen remark. They knew that life was connected to love, the most important force in the Universe. Anything artificial could never match that.

Granzo and Hashika sat quietly watching the energy flow between the elders as they discussed the way the people used brutality and violence against animals, which extended into brutality and violence within the species itself. They deliberated about the degradation and disrespect for the land, the air, and the water. They lamented the obviously decreasing intelligence of the people, who continued to choose technology over making conscious spiritual and Nature-based choices through their hearts. As they were preparing for a vote after the lengthy discussion, Hashika suddenly leaped from her seat to stand before the elders, her emerald green robe moving in waves as she positioned herself before them. She knew it was not her place to voice anything at all, but she *was* one of the two members who had actually walked among and experienced the humans. And she was touched deeply by those who exhibited higher qualities and gave off lighter and higher vibrations. Did they deserve the same treatment as the others? Didn't they deserve to be evaluated separately? No one had even considered a separate evaluation for the situation, even though it was clear to her that there was a tremendous difference between those who were exhibiting the same patterns of destructive behavior and those who appeared to be evolving as a species.

Stunned by her unexpected speech and unabashed championing of this minor number of units, or sometimes only individuals within units, the elders sat silently. Granzo shifted uncomfortably in his seat, his deep blue robe moving with him. Hashika stood tall, her hands behind her back, her eyes bright and expectant.

Silence echoed throughout the chamber. Taking a deep breath, Hashika filled the space with an unheard-of suggestion. With all eyes upon her, Hashika suggested to the Council that if the people of the planet were condemned because they could not change their behaviors, why could the Council not change its directive? Could the minor number of units not obtain a separate evaluation and receive a different treatment? Why must the Council stick to an old tradition of non-interference if it clearly wasn't working?

Now Granzo cast his eyes at the floor, after a quick reproving look at Hashika. But she did not see Granzo's warning glance. She continued to stand tall and proud, suggesting change was necessary, even in her manner of including herself in this discussion.

Finally, the eldest member of the Council rose. She, like Hashika, was tall, and every aspect of her presence radiated peace and love. Her lovely rose-colored robe rippled around her as she stood. All eyes turned to her in respect, as she slowly began to speak. "Hashika has courage and is exhibiting great wisdom. Her argument makes perfect sense," the elder stated in a calm and soothing voice.

"Why should we honor our own traditions as the only way, when clearly we can make a difference by making another choice?" She continued, "If we don't change our own methods for the highest good of all, we would be doing the same thing for which we are condemning another species. We would be abandoning them because *we* refuse to change."

The orbs in the room took on a brighter glow and began to circulate at a faster speed. Something unprecedented was definitely taking place. The elder gazed softly around the chamber, radiating love, and then took her seat. Waves of colors undulated as everyone present adjusted their energies to incorporate change. Slowly the others began to nod in agreement. Wordlessly, each of them reached agreement and silently communicated with the female elder. They were going to intervene for the minority of evolving people.

However, intervention could take many paths. Now the question for the Council had changed. If they were going to change their historical mandate of non-intervention and actually intercede in what was happening on Tehra, they must be sure that what they did was for the highest good for all. They already recognized that the decisions must be different for the minority and for the collective, for they knew that if they rescued *all* of the fractured species, most would continue their disruptive and discordant behaviors elsewhere, irresponsibly expecting that they would always be rescued from their own choices. There would be no growth. The council was realizing that it was undeniably necessary to treat the species as two separate groups, with two separate courses of action.

Once this decision had been reached, it was clear that they would abandon the experiment altogether, allowing the masses to live out the repercussions of their own choices. Because the people valued their precious technical toys more than life, they would be irradiated from effects of the satellites surrounding the planet, which saturated everything with an invisible fog of radiation. The deleterious influence would have effects on their physical, mental, and emotional health. The people's mental capacities would diminish quickly, shrinking into confusion as their physical bodies began to burn in the fires of the radiation they had created when they destroyed the protective magnetosphere around their planet through geochemical engineering—the spraying of toxic chemicals into

their skies. Cancer, heart attacks, neurological problems, and mental deterioration would be the last
things they would experience. They would expire,
as their emotions mounted in waves of unparalleled
distress and despair. They had made their choice,
and they would live and die by it. They had chosen to destroy all life on their own planet, including
their own.

But those who had evolved past selfishness,
who understood the importance of making choices
for the highest good of all, would receive the first
intervention in interstellar history. There was much
discussion about future plans and how this could
be achieved. Those they rescued would have to be
educated and then given the means to use the radiating heat they were experiencing to transform their
cells into light, as elevated species did throughout
the Universe when shape shifting from one form
to another. The education for mastering this skill
would have to be swift, for the time of planetary
annihilation was close. A team was quickly orga-
nized to work with this group of humans in the
astral realms as they meditated or slept. Those who
meditated would receive visionary guidelines as
they emerged from their meditative state. Those

who dreamed would receive the instructions in lucid dreams. The people would be given practice sessions while they were in these altered states, assuring that they understood how to initiate the process of sending light and heat into their cells with the intention of changing their forms.

These sessions would also instill the realization that those who were left behind would still receive what they needed for their own evolution —only at a slower rate and in a different place. There was no reason to grieve for those they left behind.

Once they had mastered the process in the astral realms, they would be ready to implement it to remove themselves from the dying planet at the appropriate moment. At the proper time, the team would give a signal and move in to help the trainees initiate their new skills, reminding them to intend themselves to become light and travel to the waiting ship. Direction and support would be necessary for this to work, but they had to take responsibility for doing it themselves. The team would provide assistance with the travel and in adjusting to being in a new form.

Once the Council had made the momentous decision and implemented a plan with a team to execute it, the energy all through the room seemed to change. It felt lighter and more hopeful. The orbs slowed their circular movement throughout the hall, sending out even greater waves of light, peace, and joy. Granzo and Hashika asked for permission to retire and regenerate from their mission, which was quickly granted with smiles of pleasure.

It was little more than a year after this vital Council meeting that the planet Tehra began to respond violently to the irradiating effects of the 5G, 6G, and 7G technology. Additionally, the protective barrier of the magnetosphere could no longer function to prevent the entry of harmful cosmic rays. The rays from both the sun and further afield from space now penetrated the atmosphere, directly reaching all living beings. Clouds formed containing unprecedented electrical forces that generated lightning strikes into the ground, causing the planet's core to groan and shake. Soon ripples of movement on land and in the sea progressed to unstoppable undulations and radical shaking, as Tehra shifted her position. Sharp and sudden changes on Tehra raged from the sea across the land with a vengeance. The unbearable heat from the irradiating rays increased the temperature across the planet, causing plants, animals, and people to wither and die.

The people turned to their technical devices seeking answers and solutions to their situation, but the Artificial Intelligence that was now in control ignored their pitiful online searches. The pall in the air, the crisp tingles and electrical shocks penetrating the space around them increased until it was too late to escape. Many were caught in the undertow of crumbling buildings and shifting land around them as waves of devastation engulfed them. Some managed to find safe land. After a few days, those who still lived were hungry and thirsty, but they had forgotten that Nature once provided food and drink, so they looked only in the collapsed buildings around them for what they needed, fighting for the last bottles of soda or packages of chips. Fighting and selfish to the end, most of the individuals were so intent on their own survival that they abandoned their little ones, although a few larger members clung to their small ones, simply unable to give them what they needed. The heat became more and more intense, and they burned with thirst. It was over in a matter of weeks. The planet was hot, steamy, with no sign of life anywhere. As the Council had known they would, the people had been slowly and painfully irradiated because of their own mounting unconscious choices.

But it was not the end of the species. The Council had taken action in what was to be named "The Year of Great Change." The etheric presence of the planet had been transformed to light and transported into space while the physical shell endured the choices of humans. Further, the Council had lifted the essence of various forms of life (trees, grass, plants, and animals, already of higher vibration than the humans) into a holding space to await their time of populating a New Tehra. Last of all, the handful of people who knew and understood the principal of acting for the highest good for all underwent the transmission into light and were now slowly adjusting to the transformative process on the ship above Tehra that became visible to all in the final days. Soon they would transform into the new humans on the New Tehra in a rainbow of colors that created their new, higher vibrational forms. There was a general sense of peace. These humans realized that they had earned this opportunity. They did not grieve those left behind, for they now comprehended the need for karmic lessons for those who had not obtained conscious awareness. Nor did they grieve the loss of the planet. In the process of transferring into light, great wisdom had been achieved, so they were joyful in their understanding that a New Tehra awaited them where they could live in harmony. For now, they enjoyed the hospitality and wonderful energy of everyone on the ship that was taking them to their new home.

There was a great banquet of celebration on the ship that had been overseeing the experiment on Tehra. Granzo and Hashika attended, and the new humans, who were currently in altered states of mental and physical change, were invited guests; they had the choice to remain quietly in their state of light and adjustment, or venture into a new form to participate in the celebration. Most chose to attend, although they felt as if they were in a dazed dream as they lightly moved into the room and seated themselves at tables overflowing with food and drink.

At the end of a vegan feast, there was an enormous surprise. All eyes turned to the eldest member of the Council, adorned in a deeply purple robe, as she stood and moved to the front to speak. As she graciously gazed across the room, a great peace settled over everyone. Hashika found she was holding her breath, but she didn't know why. There was a feeling of anticipation and happiness inside her. She had chosen a yellow robe today, intuitively noticing the presence of profound joy that was present in the color yellow. The elder who had led the change in policy smiled, held out her hand, and beckoned Hashika to approach. Hashika moved to stand before the older female at the front of the gathering, purple and yellow robes blending together as they lightly exchanged touch, heart to heart. Then in a tremendous surprise to everyone, with bright eyes and glowing speech, the elder announced that Hashika was invited to become a junior member of the Council for her demonstration of integrity, courage, and creative abilities. A rush of joy spilled from Hashika's heart and flowed throughout the room, radiating out to all present. Hashika smiled her acceptance and bent her head to indicate her position of learning. She would absorb much and go on to help many others realize how to live for the highest good of all. She had been an active member providing service in the Year of Great Change, and now she would serve on the Council to bring great changes to the rest of the Universe. Hashika's heart was full of joy as she stepped into her new role as a junior Council member, trusting that she would now serve in new and exciting ways as she continued to help consciousness expand in the Universe.

Exit Plan

When a whole group of people from a small country in the north disappeared, the world was startled. News reports posited political foul play or biological warfare. But it was a *very* large group of people —in fact, every single person from the western half of Swedoniaa, which was the majority of the entire Swedoniaa population, had simply disappeared in the blink of an eye. There were no reports of illness or of foreign military or dastardly political acts. These people—all of them within multiple villages throughout the entire enormous western district simply disappeared overnight. Christians spoke of the Rapture, although they were confused because these people were not of their faith. New Agers said Extra Terrestrials had taken them away, but of course, no interstellar ships were reported. Scientists and astronomers worldwide looked for a geological or cosmic event that could explain the mysterious sudden disappearance, but no meteor or weather anomaly was present to explain the occurrence. It had just happened—in a land far, far in the north to a group of people no one seemed to know much about. Everyone was puzzled—or scared.

The people of Swedoniaa who had disappeared were simple people who lived in harmony with the land and with each other. They ate only the food they grew in their own gardens and greenhouses, as all animals were considered friends, and they would never consider taking the life of an animal for food. The land was not prone to earthquakes or tsunamis or harsh weather, even though it was the northernmost continent above Europe. The sudden disappearance continued to be a mystery; no one could fathom what had caused it.

But I knew what had happened. The day they all disappeared, I felt a tingling vibration in my entire body, and my left arm shimmered in a way that I could see it, and then it disappeared, and then I could see it again. I was resonating with what was happening to the people in Swedoniaa, although at the time I had not realized it. This was possible simply because I had had a different comprehension of physical reality for a very long time. My comprehension actually began the moment I learned I could see the air, wispy strings weaving across space that fascinated me. Of course, no one else could see them. I knew from that moment that I, too, was made of parts that could not be seen, no matter how fine a microscope was employed, or how many doctors poked and prodded, trying to figure out exactly what I was made of. I may appear to look like everyone else, but I knew I was fluid, wispy, and changeable like those strings in the air. I could see things that others couldn't see, hear voices that others didn't hear, and I laughed at silent cosmic jokes that left others wondering what was so funny.

The more I learned about who I really was, the more I realized and accepted why this physical body of mine had *so* many problems. I wasn't supposed to be here. Somehow there had been a rip in the illusion of 3D physical reality, and I had found my way in, looking for someone I loved and missed who was here. He was on assignment to this planet, so I decided to find a way to be with him. It took me a year of this world's time, but I slipped through the hole, and tried to make myself invisible. Trying to make myself invisible didn't work; I guess my light was a little too bright in the dense and dull atmo-sphere of this planet, for people always noticed me. They may not have liked me, but they noticed.

Gradually I found others who were like me. Connor was the first one, of course, and then there were others. Our vibrations were different from the Earthly folk. We were empathic and able to com-municate with one another telepathically, whether we were in the same room or at a distance far apart. All of us were too conscious to consider animals as food. We felt the animals' pain, so there was abso-lutely no way we would participate in the ignorance of those who ate their meat, which added density and aggression to their vibration by doing so. Each of us had our own set of physical problems, adjust-ing to the environment that showed up in varying symptoms as we adjusted to living on planet Earth. We were also extremely sensitive to all things environmental, from simple air pollution to the fluc-tuations of solar activity in the atmosphere. If an earthquake affected one hemisphere of the planet, we would feel it in the other. Pains in our physical structure (back, head, legs, arms, and chest) reflect-ed the movement of the planet. The larger the quake, the more distress we felt in our physical bodies. A quake as large as Fukashima in Japan would bring on constriction in our chest, heart pains, and a temporary inability to move. Smaller quakes were less intense, but they still made us uncomfortable. Likewise, we struggled with physical distress from a continually higher Schumann Resonance and the cosmic rays that continued to increase during the Solar Minimum that was now in effect on the planet. Like solar flares that arrive from the sun during hotter periods, cosmic rays bring more irradiating light that is felt by the physical body as unnatural. So, when the Kp Index (showing an indication of disturbances in the Earth's magnetic field and registering the intensity of cosmic rays) showed zero protection in the magnetosphere, we were all deeply impacted. A zero Kp reading would bring mental confusion, disrupted sleep, migraine-type headaches, extreme nausea, and dizziness. In other words, it brought about non-functionality in regular Earthly activities. Even a slightly higher reading that was still below the normal 2-3 would cause burning sensations in the tissues of our eyes and mouths as the rays dried out the fluid along with a general discomfort in the body. Our bodies were being irradiated by these *intense* bursts of light.

When an extremely high Schumann Resonance was present, the higher vibration could render us almost non-functional.

I figured out, after experiencing much pain, that it was my job to find a way to let the light into my cells without acknowledging the physical distress. I realized that the only difference in pleasure or pain is our perception of the experience. I began to welcome the light and allow it to change me. After all, I came from the light, so there was no reason not to welcome it into this physical form. I created an Exit Plan, understanding that the light was changing my form, and I was going Home—back to the Light.

So, I was not surprised when an entire group of Swedoniaans had suddenly disappeared. Having visited the country of Swedoniaa once, I knew that the gentle people of that country practiced living in unity. Far to the north, they did not engage with the rest of the world very often or very much. Their conscious awareness was heightened, and their telepathic abilities were unsurpassed. Their every thought addressed the highest good for all. Therefore they had achieved their own Exit Plan, using the incoming blasts of light to change their density and lighten their bodies. Because they were united in both their thinking and their actions, they were able to accomplish a group exit. They had simply used a particularly potent blast of cosmic rays (containing so much energy that the Kp Index registered it as being "off the scale") to lighten themselves enough to instantly step into new Rainbow bodies as they left the old shells of themselves behind. The old shells, of course, disintegrated very quickly because they had no substance. The essence of the person went with the light into the new forms.

A Rainbow body is a wonderful thing! I know because I experienced it myself when I died in 2012. My new en-lightened physical form had merged with my etheric form, creating a body made of all the colors of the rainbow. In fact, the rainbow colors were all around me when I died, and I realized that they nurtured my new form. I also realized that duality ceased to exist in a Rainbow body. There was no difference between pleasure and pain because each was experienced as a passing sensation that could and would change, moment-by-moment. The reason people suffer on Earth is because of their dualistic perceptions that separate and categorize their experiences as either good or bad. In my Rainbow body, I was light and happiness and joy! But I came back to Earth in 2012 because Connor was still here, and he needed me.

I did my best to incorporate what I had learned in the Rainbow realm, but the pull of density in this reality was too great, and soon I was once again deeply immersed in the patterns of duality. Together Connor and I spent *years* working with the light, not only for our own movement into Rainbow bodies, but also to help others escape the pull and density of duality in the third dimension. We worked, as the Swedoniaan people had done, for unity and the highest good of all.

We also created our own Exit Plan, working daily to use the light to fill our cells and change our experience here on Earth. We trusted and knew that at the right moment, with a burst of light, we would use our practiced skills, and we would exit—together.

When I awoke in the night and found myself floating effortlessly downstairs (my body left in my bed), I glanced around looking for Connor. I was practiced at this, but I hadn't done it in a while. Tonight it was particularly easy. I glided through the air like I was riding on a breeze. Glancing back up the stairs, I could see the old cells of my body left behind in their shell, as my inner light grew and began to form a new body. At the foot of the stairs I saw a glow, something I remembered from my visit to the Rainbow realm. Excitedly I moved quickly towards the glow and found myself in my living room with colors and shapes and wisps of colored energy that I recognized as my true family —my star family! I remembered the feeling of warmth and love from each one of them. Looking around with appreciation, I saw that Connor was already there, too! Immediately I comprehended what was happening. This was our Exit Plan! We were using the light to take us Home, and our true family had come to escort us. We had been leaving little bits of the illusion behind us every day, as we became lighter and lighter. We had dropped everything that was not a part of our true selves, including bad moods, judgmental thoughts, and careless actions. Eliminating all those parts that were so deeply ingrained in human experience on Earth was real work, but it was worth it, for it gave us lighter and mores spacious feelings of gratitude, trust, compassion, and love. When we began to consistently live with those feelings, our distress at third-dimensional physical problems lessened, too. With our work to push against the resistance that was everywhere around us, we achieved a state of peace that allowed us to reach the vibration necessary to ascend. When others came to look for us, they would find no bodies, for I knew that the shells we left behind would quickly disintegrate. Like the Swedoniaans, we would simply appear to have vanished—our Exit Plan complete.

Afterword
Breathing Under Water

For over fifty years I have found myself repeatedly in a vivid, lucid dream state sitting on the floor of the sea, surrounded by three elder women who are very clearly teaching me how to breath under water. In each of these dreamscapes, I enter the water, going deeper and deeper until I reach the bottom where the women elders are waiting for me. In each of these dreams, I discover that I can breathe as the water closes over my head. My teachers always sit waiting for me in a circle on the bottom of the sea, smiling and beckoning me to join them.

As a younger woman, I puzzled about the meaning and guidance of these important meetings. I instinctively knew that if necessary, I *could* breath under water. In many of the dreamscapes the elders explained the similarity of water to etheric waves.

The women elders explained that they were from the stars, but they rejuvenate themselves in water here on Earth, where they have come to teach those few who are ready to remember. It was pointed out to me that the first priority for breathing under water is the absence of fear. In my dream travel, I demonstrated my lack of fear by courageously entering the water without any concern that I would not be able to breathe. And always, I was magically able to take air from the water as necessary.

The second priority, it was explained to me, is an open heart in alignment with the vibration of joy. That was absolutely no problem for me, for I always find myself laughing whenever I am in water, whether I am jumping into a freshwater lake, splashing in a creek, or diving through the waves of the ocean. I have been in touch with the vibration of joy for most of my life, although I experienced it as a fleeting thing, noticed through birdsong, a sunset, starlight, being in water, or in a sweet kiss. So, I have the two first requirements: absence of fear and a state of inner joy.

The third thing necessary was a curious imagination. I had, apparently, passed that test, too, because every day of my life I have imagined other realities that are far beyond my regular experience. Those imaginative experiences have opened me to realities much larger than my human imagination, and I am exceedingly grateful for the truth and peace I have found by accepting a larger truth than what we are taught here in our limited, third-dimensional world.

Now after receiving messages from so many wonderful voices from Love and Light throughout my life, I know that what these wonderful women elders have been teaching me in my underwater breathing lessons is the importance of waveform. Water is like etheric waveform, and the symbolism of breathing under water is the instruction on how to exist in waveform, which is where we all are going. I am grateful for these teachers, one of whom has made herself very present in my life now as Cullen and I approach our final transition into Rainbow body form, where we will be breathing in the way it has been shown to me. Her name is Moira. Because she and I are connected in this life and are also connected in parallel lives, it is quite easy for me to translate her high melodic tones and sounds into meaning with which I can resonate and share with others. The other two teachers prefer to remain anonymous, but I can see them clearly and call on them at any time. One presents to me in African form, and one presents to me as an East Indian. Moira's form shall remain a secret between us—and Cullen, of course, who knows all my secrets.

Learning to breathe and live in waveform is remembering how we can go Home. As Laarkmaa says, we simply have to remember who we are. I am thankful for Laarkmaa's years of partnership with Cullen and me on this evolutionary journey. And I am thankful for all the voices from love and light who have visited us throughout the years and particularly now as we approach a momentous evolutionary leap. Through their guidance and wisdom I have learned to be more than human. I am prepared to fulfill my role as a cosmic citizen.

The stories in this book share principles that these many wonderful voices have communicated to me. I have included stories that speak about the energy of colors, the effects of our thoughts, emotions and choices, the perils of technology, shadow work and reconciliation, the power of imagination, creativity, and manifestation, the value of transparency, our interstellar helpers, angels, and fairy realms, the necessity of releasing density and negativity, the value of integrating parallel lives, how to live through the principles of *In Lak'ech* and *Ahimsa*, the possibilities that exist for each of us, how to remember who we are, the importance of non-attachment and letting go, and a view of our final transition into waveform. I hope you have enjoyed my stories and that they have been meaningful to you. It is my wish that each of you who has read this book use your own imagination, creativity, and your remembering to help bring more consciousness to the world.

Acknowledgments

My first acknowledgment is to my spiritual sister, Vineta Svelch, who made the production of this book possible. When she read my stories, she told me, "Your stories need to be published so that they, like Mary's woven fabric of Light, inspire all the readers and help them remember who they truly are!" As a linguist and writer herself, Vineta's gentle but brilliant editorial notes and beautiful organizational suggestions were invaluable, and her insistence that the book be made public made this happen. Thank you, Vineta, for your love, your support, and for investing in me. You are responsible for making a dream come true!

My heartfelt gratitude to my cosmic partner, Cullen Baird Smith, who read my stories first. Your critical eye provided suggestions for filling in the gaps and cutting out unnecessary repetition. Your comments kept me from wandering off the page with my thoughts. I treasure your eternal care for me and my projects.

I am privileged to use the original artwork created by my friend Anna Karmaz for the cover of this book. Anna, you are a brilliant artist, and I am honored that you offered to create an original piece of art to reflect the feeling of my stories. It felt like magic the minute you became involved in my book, and your art clearly reflects the essence of my stories!

To Brendan and Diann Bowen, your corrections of punctuation and spelling, your scientific suggestions, your cosmic awareness, and your vision were most useful in fine-tuning these stories. Thank you. Your friendship is even more valuable than your editing talents!

I thank Rebecca Finkel for her relentless work with me to create the perfect cover and book layout. Your fresh approach was just what my stories needed to introduce them to the world!

Finally, I thank all the voices, both otherworldly and human, who provided the inspiration to tell these tales.

Wisdom from the Stars Trilogy

Here are three inspiring books by Pia Orleane and Cullen Baird Smith full of Pleiadian wisdom from Laarkmaa!

Book 1:

Conversations with Laarkmaa —
A Pleiadian View of the New Reality

For the first time in history, a Pleiadian group has invited a human couple to join an interplanetary team for helping the evolution of humanity.

Cullen Baird Smith and Pia Orleane, Ph.D., acting as ambassadors to the Pleiadians, bring Laarkmaa's inspiring and heart warming messages of hope, love, and peace to all those who are

willing to listen. Through recorded conversations with this Pleiadian group, Orleane and Smith share Laarkmaa's wisdom about the coming changes, the illusion of time, the future of technology, our innate ability to heal ourselves, the power of our thoughs, and information about who is here to guide us through this auspicious time. Laarkmaa is equally interested in speaking to us and hearing our responses. The dialogue includes their questions to humanity, such as, "What do humans need?" "How can we support you?" and "How can we help you to choose the right path?" The ensuing conversations bring revelatory insights about human emotions, telepathic communications, and our own divinity. The Pleiadians tell us that we have a choice in changing the course of our own evolution. Will we make the right choice?

Available at www.laarkmaa.com

Book 2:

Remembering Who We Are— Laarkmaa's Guidance on Healing the Human Condition

Laarkmaa's Pleiadian dedication to the evolution of humanity continues in *Remembering Who We Are*. Laarkmaa shares amazing insights on how we

can heal ourselves from all our discomfort and disease. Guiding us towards unimaginable possibilities, Laarkmaa shares wisdom about the nature of energy, the polarities of fear and love, our life purpose, the power of speech, the illusion of time, how to heal our relationships, and how we can manifest a better world. Each truth they share builds upon a preceding insight, until we are ultimately given all of the tools we need to heal ourselves and our world. The reader arriveds at the end of the journey to find a series of choices. Will we, individually and collectively, make the right choices for our own evolution?

Available at www.laarkmaa.com

Book 3: Pleiadian Manual
for Accelearted Evolution & Ascension—
Laarkmaa's Step By Step Guide

In this last book of the *Wisdom From the Stars* Trilogy, Laarkmaa gives us the guidelines and their suggestions for moving through our own evolution 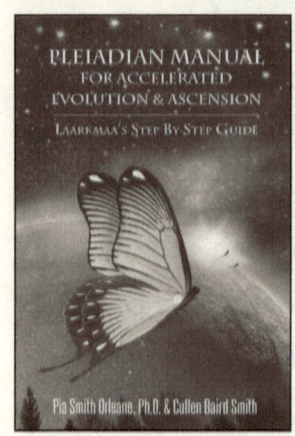 and ascension with flexibility, flow, and grace. Explaining the changing structures of our world and offering ways to prepare for this transition, the Manual provided by these interstellar friends helps humanity to move beyond the illusion of the third dimension into a greater multidimensional perspective of reality. Important topics covered in this book include a comprehensive description of consciousness, suggestions for an Ascension Diet, the Cosmic Weather, a surprising definition of the Dark, the effects of Light, and a wonderful description of unconditional love. The final chapter leads us into the secrets of manifestation.

Available at www.laarkmaa.com

Pleiadian-Earth Energy Astrology—Charting the Spirals of Conscouisness

2019 COVR Award Winner for Divination!

Discover how to navigate the spiral energy patterns of the universe for spiritual advancement and conscious evolution

Modern science has finally confirmed an essential component of the Pleiadian teachings: Our Universe is not linear; it moves in spirals. Human evolution also unfolds in spirals, rather than the linear progression we call "progress." Sharing the cosmic wisdom teachings, they have received from the Pleiadian group known as Laarkmaa, authors Pia Orleane and Cullen Baird Smith reveal a new system of Pleiadian-Earth Energy Astrology centered on the spiraling and interconnected movement of Universal and Earth energies, rather than on time. This book explains how this new wave of Pleiadian wisdom can support human evolution.

The authors identify two major spiral patterns that influence us: the 13 spirals of Universal energy that reflect cosmic laws and cosmic truth and the 20 spirals of Earth energy that reflect how humans experience themselves, each other, and their environment. They explain the dominant energy of each of the 13 Universal energy spirals and how they cycle in 13-day periods. They detail how these 13 Universal energy spirals interact with the cycles of the 20 Earth energy spirals on each calendar day, providing an ephemeris of Gregorian dates and a Pleiadian perspective with which to understand the events in your life. Offering practical examples, they show how you can consciously use the energies prevalent on a given calendar day to your personal, spiritual advantage.

Providing a map to transcend all systems that no longer serve us, freeing us to become the enlightened cosmic beings we truly are, the authors show how, with the wisdom of the Pleiadian-Earth energy system, we can each discover our specific gifts, work through the challenges of our own shadows, and individually and collectively evolve into a higher vibrational species.

Sacred Retreat—
Using Natural Cycles
to Recharge Your Life

2017 Gold Nautilus Award Winner!

All of life is interwoven into a living system of cycles, from Earth's seasons to the enzymatic pathways that provide energy to a cell. Waxing and waning from times of growth to times of rest, renewal, and healing, cycles map the most auspicious time for everything in life. Both women and men have biological cycles of active growth and quiet renewal, led by our hormones. By understanding how everything in life moves in cycles, you can become more aware of and comfortable with your own cyclic nature, something that has been forgotten by the modern world's linear views of time.

Drawing on the wisdom of ancient cultures, the natural cycles of life, and her own groundbreaking research, Pia Orleane, Ph.D., offers a template for how we can restore balance to our emotions and health, ease tensions between the genders, and heal our fractured culture by honoring divine feminine consciousness and re-embracing natural cycles, including our innate need for rest and retreat. She explains the biology of how our bodies operate by hormones released in cycles and shows how balanced hormones help eliminate anger, depression, insomnia, anxiety, and fatigue. Exploring ancient traditions and rituals surrounding blood and sacred retreat, she explains how the seclusion of women during menstruation and of men during vision quests offered a cleansing process for body and mind and alone time to clear suppressed emotions, awaken our innate creativity and sensitivity, re-attune with the deeper rhythms of nature, and restore harmony between the genders.

Outlining the sacred retreat process, the author explores dream cycles, divine sexuality, and practices for reconnecting to nature, increasing creativity and intuition, and clearing suppressed emotions. She also looks at the benefits for women and men of separate sleeping during menstruation. Through this wisdom, we can restore our natural cycles, allow the divine feminine to once again blossom alongside the divine masculine, and with the return of balance, heal our world and our hearts.

Available at InnerTraditions.com

Southern Piercings

Coalition for Visionary Fiction 2012 Award Winner!

When a phone call from Georgia summons Jenny on a spiritual journey through her past, she forges the courage to face her inner conflicts. Prodded by her angels and gathering strength from Nature, Jenny begins a journey unlike any other. This time, she is determined to escape the grasp of her mother and her feelings of hopelessness in order to redeem her own life.

In *Southern Piercings,* Pia Orleane has given us a novel full of hope and spiritual insights. Through Jenny's story, Dr. Orleane reveals secrets for reaching beyond the lifelong patterns of trauma that cripple us, teaching us how to move beyond and transcend pain to reach true fulfillment.

This novel is currently being updated and revised.

About the Author

Pia Orleane, Ph.D. has been called a Receiver of Universal Wisdom. Awarded a Ph.D. in Psychology (specialty: Consciousness Studies) by Saybrook University, the former practicing psychologist is a respected intuitive, author, and creator of the revelatory *Pleiadian-Earth Energy Astrology* system. She was given a grant for groundbreaking research, which she used to turn her research into the book *Sacred Retreat—Using Natural Cycles to Recharge Your Life,* which won the Nautilus Gold Book Award. Several of Pia's books have been published in English, French, German, Italian, Russian, and Chinese.

This is Pia's second work of fiction. (The first, a novel that won the COVR Award for Visionary Fiction, is currently being revised.) This book of stories is based on Pleiadian perspectives and wisdom she has "received" from other voices from the light.

Pia is co-author with her husband, Cullen Baird Smith, of four books on human evolution listed earlier in this book. Together they work with the Pleiadian group, Laarkmaa, bringing a larger view of the true reality to the world. It is Cullen who first called Pia a Receiver as the many voices from love and light spoke through her. Pia and Cullen currently live in Europe. You can find out more about her work at **PiaOrleane.com** or **laarkmaa.com**

www.ingramcontent.com/pod-product-compliance
Lightning Source LLC
Chambersburg PA
CBHW022024120726
47898CB00007BA/2139